Rumplestiltskin

JENNI JAMES

Village Lane Publishing

PRAISE FOR JENNI JAMES

Beauty and the Beast (Faerie Tale Collection)

"Jenni James takes this well-loved faerie tale and gives it a paranormal twist. Very well-written and hard to put down, even on my cruise vacation where I had plenty to do. Looking forward to others in Jenni's Faerie Tale series. A great escape!"
—Amazon reviewer, 5-star review

Pride & Popularity (The Jane Austen Diaries)

"This book was unputdownable. I highly recommend it to any fan of Jane Austen, young or old. Impatiently awaiting the rest of the series."
—Jenny Ellis, Librarian and Jane Austen Society of North America

"Having read several other young adult retellings of *Pride and Prejudice,* I must admit that *Pride and Popularity* by Jenni

James is my top choice and receives my highest recommendation! In my opinion, it is the most plausible, accessible, and well-crafted YA version of *Pride and Prejudice* I have read! I can hardly wait to read the [next] installment in this series!"

—Meredith, *Austenesque Reviews*

"I started reading *Pride and Popularity* and couldn't put it down! I stayed up until 1:30 in the morning to finish. I've never been happier to lose sleep. I was still happy this morning. You can't help but be happy when reading this feel-good book. Thank you, Jenni, for the fun night!"

—*Clean Teen Fiction*

Northanger Alibi (The Jane Austen Diaries)

"*Twilight*-obsessed teens (and their moms) will relate to Claire's longing for the fantastical, but will be surprised when they find the hero is even better than a vampire or werewolf. Hilarious, fun, and romantic!"

Prince Tennyson

"After reading *Prince Tennyson*, your heart will be warmed, tears will be shed, and loved ones will be more appreciated. Jenni James has written a story that will make you believe in miracles and tender mercies from above."
—Sheila Staley, book reviewer and writer

"Divinely inspired, beautifully written—a must read!"
—Gerald D. Benally, author of *Premonition (2014)*

"*Prince Tennyson* is a sweet story that will put tears in your eyes and hope in your heart at the same time."
—Author Shanti Krishnamurty

Village Lane Publishing
Utah, Idaho, Germany
www.VillageLanePublishing.com

First eBook Edition: 2013
First Paperback Edition: 2013

Second eBook edition: 2019
Second Paperback Edition: 2019
ISBN: 978-1-951496-98-2

Cover design by Phatpuppy Art

Published in the United States of America

Village Lane Publishing, LLC

ALSO BY JENNI JAMES

Jenni James Faerie Tale Collection:
Beauty and the Beast
Sleeping Beauty
Cinderella
Snow White
Hansel and Gretel
Jack and the Beanstalk
The Frog Prince
The Twelve Dancing Princesses
Rapunzel
The Little Mermaid
Rumplestiltskin
Peter Pan
Return to Neverland
Captain Hook

The Jane Austen Diaries:
Pride & Popularity
Northanger Alibi
Persuaded
Emmalee
Mansfield Ranch
Sensible & Sensational

Prince Tennyson
Revitalizing Jane

Regency Romance Series
The Bluestocking and the Dastardly,
Intolerable Scoundrel
Lord Romney's Exquisite Widow
Lord Atten Meets His Match

Modern Fairy Tales
Not Cinderella's Type
Beauty IS the Beast
Sleeping Beauty: Back to Reality
The Shattered Slipper

ACKNOWLEDGMENTS

I WOULD LIKE TO thank Carola Dunn for her version of *Rumplestiltskin* that I first read in a fairy tale collection of Regency authors titled *Once Upon a Time*. Her story was the first time I had ever seen the concept of Rumplestiltskin being the hero who was crippled. And so, the spark of my Rumple was born years ago. When Aaron Patterson asked me to write fairy tales for him, I knew I would have to do my own version of Rumplestiltskin using the idea from Carola Dunn that indeed Rumplestiltskin was the true hero.

And a huge thank you to the wonderful Claudia Lucia McKinney. Without her gorgeous artwork, my covers for the Faerie Tale Collection would be nothing. I love you! You are wonderful.

And as always, the divine inspiration given to help me create such amazing parables.

x

*This book is dedicated to my own
real-life Rumplestiltskin,
Layton Fredrick,
who was paralyzed ten years ago.*

*Your constant cheerfulness and humor
through excessive trials raise me up and
give me courage I never knew I had.
You are a true modern-day hero
and I am blessed to know you and love
you. Thank you for all your words
of encouragement. Thank you for your
hours of laughter. Thank you
for saving me. But mostly, thank you for
giving me the magic to turn
my words into gold and share this
message with the world. You are
beautiful, and you shine brighter than
anyone I know.*

Rumplestiltskin

CHAPTER ONE

HIS ROYAL HIGHNESS FREDERICO Baldrich Layton's little legs ran fast—faster than they had ever traveled before. Soon he would be at the meadow, the pretty one with the magic pond. If he could just get there before Nurse Crabtree did, he knew he could collect the strange, small rocks and stuff them into his pockets and she would never know.

She did not let him bring the pebbles back yesterday when they had played at the magic pond. It was now or never, while she was sipping her tea and talking to the Reverend Townesend. Now was the time to dash to the pond and bring back those amazing stones.

He could hardly wait to show his baby brother. Marcus was only three, but he sure did love rocks, especially strange rocks.

Frederico rounded the corner past the old willow tree and skidded to a halt. Glancing back through the hanging branches, he saw Nurse Crabtree all the way across the field, still talking with the reverend.

"Good!" She had not even noticed he was missing yet. Without another thought, he rushed past the blackberry bushes, over to the pond, to the special spot where he had been told to set the stones down.

"They are still here!"

Quickly, he collected all six of the odd, shiny black-and-blue striped rocks and stuffed them into his coat pocket. Then, just as he was about to rush back to

Nurse Crabtree, he heard a shuffling in the bushes. Turning toward the sound, he was surprised to see a crooked old lady step out of them.

"Do you live in there?" he asked before remembering it was not polite to speak until spoken to.

"No, I do not," barked the old woman as she glanced around. "Where do you live, young man? And how old are you? You do not look old enough to be scampering about alone."

Prince Frederico stood to his full height, his little chest puffed out like he had seen his father, the king, do many times and said, "I am five, and I live in the castle over there." He pointed to the large fortress.

"Do you?" The old woman seemed very interested. "Whose castle is it?"

"My father, King Albert's, of course."

The old woman's eyes snapped to his and she looked long and hard at the young boy before asking, "Are you certain King Albert lives there?"

"Yes, ma'am."

"Are you his heir, then?"

"Yes, I am!" he stated proudly.

She surprised him by spitting on the ground. Some of the spittle landed upon his shiny kid-leather boots. Frederico backed a few paces away.

"Well, it is a sad day indeed. You seem like a nice, hardy lad—however, your family is pure evil, and I will not stand to have this land ruined. Just twenty years ago, your grandfather ruled with kindness as a perfect example to all, but now your father and mother have nearly brought the kingdom to its knees with their selfish taxes and uncaring practices. Therefore, I am sorry to say, they must be taught a lesson, and it will be through you that I choose to do it."

"Through me?" asked Frederico, not quite certain what she was speaking about.

"Yes, boy. Come here quickly, before they find you missing and come after their little jewel."

"I—"

"Come, lad. Now." She held her hand out and grasped his tiny fingers, pulling him sharply behind the bush. Before he even knew what was happening, she mumbled several incoherent words over him and watched, satisfied, as his face contorted with pain.

"It is for your own good, my boy, for the good of us all. You will see."

And that was that.

She shoved him out from under the bushes and disappeared in a poof of smoke.

Confused, the young prince attempted to head back to his nurse. He was hurting. His fingers were all twisted and bent, and so was his body. One foot would not even move anymore. All he wanted was to return home and feel better again.

As quickly as his crippled body could take him, dragging his unusable foot the whole way, he burst into the garden and interrupted tea time with the reverend.

Nurse Crabtree screamed and shattered her cup upon the table as she jumped up to get away from him.

Reverend Townesend placed an arm over her and another out toward the young boy. "Do not come another step closer, do you hear? Do not do it."

Big tears began to build within Frederico. He had been so brave until now, but when Nurse screamed, it frightened him. "Help me." He tried to walk closer, but she only moved farther away. "Help me."

"You—you are cursed! You will make us all cursed!" Nurse Crabtree shouted.

"Help me, please!"

"Stay right there until I send someone for you." The reverend took the nurse by the hand and walked toward the castle. On his way, he hollered at a maidservant who was just exiting with her arms full of new refreshments for their tea. "Get the prince and take him to his room. Do not let anyone see him. Do you understand?"

"Yes, sir." The maid curtsied and scurried over to Frederico.

He would never forget the terror in her eyes or the scream she let out when she first beheld his crippled form. The boy had no idea how awful he looked, but it made him cry so much more to see her fear.

She stepped back a pace and pointed. "What happened to you? Your skin is all rumpled and stilted."

"A woman hurt me. I don't know why—I did nothing to her."

6

"A woman?" She came forward. "A woman did this to you? Was she on the grounds? Where was she?"

"Over by the lake. I came as fast as I could."

"Just a few moments ago?"

"Yes."

"I will be back. Wait right here—no one can see you like this!"

***

The maid gathered her skirts and ran as fast as she could to the head gardener and told him she had seen a strange woman walking the grounds who needed to be caught and brought to the king. When she got back, little Frederico was sitting upon the ground, his head in his bent hands, staring at the grass.

"Come on, little one. Let us get you back to the palace and washed up."

Frederico rubbed his eyes with a crooked fist, sniffled, and looked up at the maid. She flinched a little, but did not scream again. It looked like she had become a little less scared as he scrambled to his feet. "When can I get better?"

"Soon. Very soon. But first, we must get you all cleaned up. I am sure the king and queen will want to see what has happened to you."

The maid was afraid of the curse, but the little boy's wet eyes checked her. Hesitantly, she reached out her hand for him to hold and prayed nothing bad would happen to her.

Frederico smiled a crooked smile and clasped her hand tight.

Her eyes were wide, but she put a brave grin on her face as she began to walk back with the little prince. "Do not look at anyone right now. And be sure to walk as straight as possible. Try not to make a scene. We will head through the back door and up the servants' entrance. Can you do that for me?"

"Yes. I think so."

She could tell he tried to walk normally, but a rolling gait was all he could accomplish. Thankfully, they made it into the castle without anyone noticing.

Once they were in his room, it was just a few minutes to get the little boy undressed and in the bath. The maid pressed her lips together many a time and tried desperately not to sob at the sight of the ruined little body. He had been so beautiful before, so lively and handsome. Now his whole person was deformed, rumpled and crippled. She closed her eyes to the protruding, awkward bones that formed his crooked back and hummed a small song instead as she poured bathwater over his head.

> *Bathing the baby.*
> *Bathing the boy.*
> *Bathing the master's dog*
> *And its toy.*

> *Soon they will be all clean as a whistle*
> *Ready to scamper about in the thistle.*

> *Bathing the baby.*
> *Bathing the boy.*
> *Bathing the master's dog.*
> *What a joy!*

***

Frederico liked that song. He hummed along with the maid the whole rest of the time it took to get dried off and dressed with socks and boots on. She was very nice. When she was brushing out his hair, he asked her, "What is your name?"

Surprised, she looked down at his distorted features. "Why do you ask?"

"Mamma always calls you 'maid.' Do you have a name?"

"Of course I have a name, Your Highness! Everyone has a name."

"Do you know my name?"

She chuckled. "Yes. Everyone better know your name if they know what's good for 'em."

"Then what is yours? I want to know yours."

She looked at him a very long time and then said, "Tilly, my little Rumple-stilt-skin. My name is Tilly."

CHAPTER TWO

IT HAD BEEN NEARLY eighteen years since Rumplestiltskin had been transformed. Eighteen years since the five-year-old Frederico had died and they buried a box full of his old clothes and dirt deep within the ground. The headstone read:

**HERE LIES OUR BELOVED PRINCE
MAY HE REST IN PEACE FOREVER**

HRH FREDERICO BALDRICH LAYTON

Rumplestiltskin pushed away from the windowsill in disgust. His mother, the queen, was having the servants prepare his grave for the annual mourning prayer they were to have in two days' time.

Some years he would stand there and chuckle to himself, watching them sobbing, but this year—this year he could not bear to watch the preparations for an event that had never occurred. It hurt this year for some reason. It hurt much more than most years.

He clutched his oiled cloth, hobbled to the gleaming surface of the tabletop, and began to shine it once again while trying to shut out that day from his memory altogether—the day his mother and father had decided to announce his death to the kingdom and disown him. Gone were his favorite toys and soft bed. All those things were saved for his brother Marcus.

Rumplestiltskin rubbed more vigorously. It was sad to see how changed his brother had become. Marcus did not deserve to be king. He was cruel to the peasants and treated everyone as if they were filth to be scraped off his boot.

Rumplestiltskin pulled back and hunched down, his left foot twisting wildly behind him as he began to polish the legs of the table. Of course, his brother had learned everything from their father. How grateful Rumplestiltskin had been to see him buried! He had no idea how brutal his father could be until Rumple's deformities made it impossible to recognize the boy as the prince, his son. As soon as his father declared he was too hideous to be considered royalty and therefore should be taken from his sight, Frederico truly died, and he began to think of himself as rumpled and stilted.

His little heart had broken in two. For weeks, he'd wept in the tiny back cellar under the kitchen floor. Thank goodness for Tilly and her kind heart! She proved to be his biggest ally back then and risked her job and life many a time to see that her little Rumplestiltskin was fed and clothed.

She would even sneak into Marcus's room and gather old, abandoned broken toys for Rumplestiltskin to play with. He had a new pile of straw brought in every few months from the stables, and Tilly and the other women patched him up a royal quilt from the fine, discarded clothing for his blanket each Christmas.

Rumplestiltskin had hidden in the castle so long, working as best he could to ease the demands of his parents and now his brother, that he truly did not remember much of the time before his servitude began. It was all a blur.

His family knew he was living in the castle somewhere. He would see them stare at him from time to time and then blankly turn away. His mother's horrified sneers had grown fewer over the years, and since his father had died, he had been seen more and more as a servant and not as an awful curse. There had been times when, if the king saw him, he had just moments to escape back to the small cellar before the guards searched the premises for him. He did not come up often when the royal family was about in those days. However, now he was simply Rumplestiltskin, no one but the crippled servant whose world they would not acknowledge or deem worthy of their notice.

Rumple rubbed harder at the beautiful wooden legs of the table, paying particular attention to the clawed feet. He had hours to think and perfect his wood-shining abilities. Hours to hide unnoticed in a room somewhere and polish and polish until everything in that room gleamed.

He did not mind working, though it hurt him greatly on days when his rheumatism was acting up and his joints did not respond as he wished. However, it gave him purpose—something to do that would beautify his beloved home.

Though the castle was not his anymore, it was still the home he lived in, and he took great pride in seeing it stunningly on display. Nevertheless, today was a day more full of despair than pride. Today pierced his heart and wounded his crippled frame more than he had felt in years.

In two days' time, all the villagers would come once again to weep over his false grave, to lament over his early death. All of them would come at Marcus's insistence, but none would truly be there because they cared. No, they were more frightened of what would happen if they did not show proper respect.

They were sore afraid of King Marcus. Even his mother was fearful of him. And yet, they pretended to love a boy they discarded years ago.

It was all a mockery. A sham!

His mother and brother could not have cared less, and the villagers honestly wished themselves miles away from their duties. No one wanted him. No one would ever want him again. And certainly no one wished to mourn for him, either.

Tilly had left specific orders to the groomsmen and womenfolk to continue to provide fresh hay and create quilts for him as she lay upon her sickbed last year. She had made them all promise they would continue to love and protect her Rumplestiltskin, but she was gone now. He had gained favor with the servants and groomsmen and the like. He had. They all respected his quiet, hardworking, cheerful ways. But they still revered him and feared him more than truly loved him, as Tilly had.

Perhaps that was why it was so hard this year to bear the silliness that would happen below. Tilly would not be there to wrap her arm around his shoulder later that night and jest and mock all the patrons who had come.

How she would make him laugh! His chuckles at her remembered antics would keep him up many a night afterward, thinking of the oddity of it all.

How Tilly had loved him!

How she truly cared about her little rumpled boy.

What would he have done without her?

What in the world would he do now that she was gone?

Rumple crawled over to the wall nearest him and swung his crooked legs around so his sore back leaned against the elegant gold-and-maroon wallpaper. He dipped his head into his arms, the dirty polishing rag still dangling from his fingers, and wept.

He did not cry when she had passed on nearly a year ago. He had remained brave and true, as she had requested.

Yet now—now he was not so brave anymore. Now her love that had sustained him had grown as cold as the ground she was buried in. He needed his Tilly. This grown man wept for the only true mother he had ever known as if he were just the boy of five she had found all those years ago and not three and twenty.

Rumple's shoulders shook as he wept, his tears plopping in great smacks onto the lustrous marble.

It was some time before he could recall himself to where he was, and even some time much later before he could shake the feeling of helplessness and extreme sorrow from his thoughts. Eventually, the forgotten prince worked his way down the steps into the kitchen, past the scurrying servants, and into his room below. He tossed the old coat off his shoulders and slumped onto the straw-matted bed. His fingers wove themselves into the silken blanket Tilly had commissioned for him and slowly, pulling the soft fabric up over himself, he curled his jagged legs as tight as he could and wondered if he would ever know such warmth and laughter again.

He had long ago given up the thought of any woman falling in love with him. He knew he would never have a family, children, or a true life of his own, but then, it had all seemed fine with Tilly around to cheer him. Now, his future was unsettled, so completely unsure, and undoubtedly full of intense loneliness forevermore.

His eyes roamed the ramshackle room, lovingly taking in every bit of Tilly that she had left for him. The old pictures she had purloined from the attics, the mock windowsill and draperies she had fastened out of several pieces of fabric and arranged over the large landscape paintings to create his own outside world. The ornaments and bejeweled cases she had found and fixed for him. The old clock, the battered toys, the candlesticks, the piles of papers and ink quills and the books she had managed to collect for him. They were all there. All upon old, forgotten furniture and crates she had amassed over the years.

Oh, how she loved him! How she tried so very hard to make his life as happy as possible. And she truly did. She was a saint, an angel sent to lift his burdens and help carry him through everything.

Another tear crept down Rumple's cheek as he sniffed his final sniff and accepted once and for all that he would never be as wholly and perfectly loved again.

He was a curse. A nuisance. A crippled man.

He did not deserve the love of others.

He was Rumplestiltskin.

CHAPTER THREE

ON THE DAY OF the commemoration of Prince Frederico's death, Aubrynn Sloat hustled and bustled around the small cottage to prepare for the trip up to the castle grounds. It was imperative that every villager attend or the king's men would be sure to toss them in the dungeons. It was used as a day of reckoning—of final tax collecting and an accounting of all the villagers still under the king's reign.

Aubrynn groaned for the third time as she placed her lunch and her father's into the knapsack. Two apples, bread, and a chunk of cheese. Yet where was her father?

Did he not know the time? He should have returned hours ago—last night even, and yet, here it was morning and still no sign of him.

Many of their neighbors had already begun the trek to the top of the mountain. She would have to leave soon, or she would be late.

Aubrynn collected the few coins she had managed to hide from her father for the taxes and tucked them safely into the pocket of her petticoat. She gathered up the water cups and placed them in the knapsack and then tapped her foot— waiting. Another ten minutes had her glancing at the final crowds making their way past the window.

She must leave. Heaven knew where her father was this time, which tavern he had decided to attend last evening. It could not be helped. She could not wait another moment. Already she would have to rush to catch up to the last of them.

Grabbing her shawl, she threw it around her shoulders as she clutched the knapsack and dashed out the door. She fumbled with the lock as she closed the cottage up and scanned the small yard. No sign of her father anywhere. Anxiety plagued Aubrynn, and for a moment she felt she would be ill. How foolish could her father be? And today of all days!

With another glance around, she scurried to catch up to the last of the families already yards ahead of her.

Her trek took just under an hour. It was nearly impossible to keep her skirts from being covered in mud due to the rain the night before. It would seem the Fates had guaranteed that anything and everything would go wrong this day.

Aubrynn sighed and hitched her skirts as high as she dared while still appearing modest and climbed the last of thc stone steps leading to the back of the castle gardens. Most everyone had already paid their respects and taxes, and they were now gathered en masse by the royal tombstones.

She tried not to show her nervousness as she turned her back on the crowd, removed the coins from her petticoat, and made her way to the guards in charge of collecting the taxes. The very last to approach them, she held out her money.

"Yer name, miss?"

"Aubrynn and Daniel Sloat."

The man scrolled through the list of hundreds of names. "Daniel yer father?"

"Yes, sir."

The man looked up. "Where is he, then?"

"I, uh . . ." Aubrynn flushed. "I am afraid he had to relieve himself. He could not wait a moment longer."

"All people must be accounted for. You tell yer father to come here after this is over so that I may be sure to cross him off this list. All those not crossed off meet an outcome they are not too eager to experience." His kind eyes met hers. "You will find yer father soon, yes?"

"I—uh, yes. I hope so."

"See that you do. It is orders we cannot disobey."

"Yes, sir. I know. Thank you." She dipped a curtsy and hurried away, praying silently her father showed up despite himself.

Already the musicians had begun their tribute to the deceased prince as Aubrynn stepped up to the end of the crowd. Men and women alike were wiping their eyes and attempting all manner of whimpers to appease the royal family. She caught a glimpse of the beautifully dressed queen as the multitude parted. King Marcus stood to deliver his speech.

Aubrynn looked down with the others, not willing to meet the man's eyes. She stared at the stones around her feet, allowing his words to glide over her, only catching about every third one. Soon this would all be over. Soon she could head home and wait until they were summoned next year.

But if her father did not come, she was not sure she would even have a house to live in until next year. Without her father in the home, the king would surely take it. Where would she go? Her mother's sister lived about fifty miles south in a neighboring kingdom; perhaps she would take her in? Or if she offered herself as a maid for free room and board, maybe one of her own neighbors would take her? But no one could afford the luxury of another mouth to feed. Things were tight everywhere with the king's high taxes.

Aubrynn cringed and took a deep breath, chanting within her mind, "Please come, Father. Please come, Father. Please come, Father . . ." over and over again until she thought her heart would burst. Heaven knew he had never been a good father, not even while her mother and sister were still alive, but since their deaths, he had gone completely downhill.

It was as if Mother's presence had kept him in check just long enough to be halfway respectable. Now the man was a drunkard, plain and simple. He spent way too much on drink and slothed away the rest of the hours until his next bottle, leaving the house and farm work to his daughter.

She was lost so deep in thought, it was a few minutes before she noticed the commotion coming from the opposite end of the gathering. It was not until the group jostled and stepped back that she was even aware there was a disturbance.

Standing on tiptoe, she could not make out more than the shoulders and heads of all those around her, but with a glance toward the king, she could tell from the look upon his face that he was greatly displeased.

"You there!" he shouted. "Come up to the front at once."

Aubrynn could just see the red feathers of the guards' helmets as they moved through the mass to the front of the podium. The guards stopped right below the king. Everyone around her was straining to hear and see what was going on as they bumped her aside.

"Why have you come to disturb my brother's memorial? What is it you were shouting out there?"

"'Tis a man they have!" whispered a woman next to her.

"Who is it? What is he saying?" came the whispered responses all around her.

"Shh. I cannot make out what is being said."

"What is your name?" bellowed the king. His head dipped out of sight, clearly to hear the man they had captured. It was several moments before the king stood back up. "Is that so?" He seemed taken aback.

"What did he say? What did he say?" whispered another villager.

"Shh!"

The king shook his head and then announced loudly, "If that is so, I allow you a moment to come up to the stand and talk with me."

The crowd surged again and Aubrynn watched as the guards brought a man up the steps of the podium and toward the king. She could barely make out the back of the man's head as he bowed low and began to speak, but the coat jacket he wore—that jacket she would know anywhere.

"Father!" Just as quickly as her heart soared that he had come, it dropped. What was he doing?

Suddenly, the king's voice rang loud and clear. "Aubrynn Sloat, if you are within this company, I command you to show yourself at once."

CHAPTER FOUR

LARGE GASPS AND MURMURS broke out all around Aubrynn as she nervously stepped forward. Slowly, she made her way through the crowd and up to the podium, where her father grinned down at her.

"This is my daughter!" He smiled and pointed toward her as she curtsied. "She is the one I have been telling you about. I promise, Yer Majesty, you will be very pleased with her!" He took a step to the left and swayed a bit.

Aubrynn's whole body went cold. Her father was clearly intoxicated. What had he said about her? What had happened?

The king's eyes roamed over Aubrynn, his head tilting to the side slightly. "Come up here and speak with me." He gestured toward the steps, and one of the guards was quick to come to her aid and help her up them. He held tightly onto her, as if he was afraid she would run.

Oh, how she wished she could run! Instead, she dipped into a formal curtsy before the young king.

* * *

Rumple hurried away from the window and out of the room as soon as the king called the girl forward. He managed to make his way outside and hide behind the bushes just as she curtsied again before the king. He was as curious as everyone else as to why the king would call the maiden before him.

From the stiff way she had stepped back, he could tell she was terrified. Perhaps she did not know what was happening either.

Fidgeting, she glanced away from the king and toward the bush where he was hidden, perhaps twelve or so feet away.

My! She is beautiful.
Scared, but oh, so beautiful.

He was lost in his thoughts for a moment and did not hear the words his brother spoke straight away.

"Forgive me, Your Majesty, but what did you say?" asked the girl, glancing nervously around her. The size of the group of people must have been completely overwhelming.

"I asked if it was true, this gift of yours that your father has been boasting about."

"Gift?"

"Yes!" King Marcus was beginning to lose his temper. "Can you or can you not spin straw into gold?"

"What?" The girl's face went white and she stumbled a bit.

Rumple watched the girl's frightened eyes as they flew to her father, imploring him to make sense of all this and explain himself.

"Yes, she can!" The man lurched forward and thumped his daughter upon the back. "This here girl of mine is a magical being. You would be a fool indeed not to want her for yer wife!"

"Father!" Aubrynn reddened, her hands visibly shaking.

"Is what your father says true, girl?" Marcus stepped forward, his finger lifting her chin up to study her features.

She flinched slightly, but otherwise remained stiff, refusing to answer.

Clearly, she had no magical abilities whatsoever. "Lie to him," Rumple whispered quietly to himself. "Lie. Tell the most convincing falsehood you can."

The king clenched the girl's jaw. "Tell me now. Can you turn straw into gold?"

Rumple sucked in air and tightened his hold upon the nearest branch.

She closed her eyes and nodded.

Heaving a sigh of relief, Rumple watched as his brother began to lightly stroke her jaw and neck.

"Good. Because if you can, I *will* marry you."

Her eyes closed tightly, obviously repulsed by his forward behavior as his hand moved to her shoulder and clasped it.

"But if you are lying and cannot do what your father says you can, he will die."

The girl's eyes flew to the king, and for a moment she looked just like a frightened rabbit facing a hunter before she nodded again.

"You are very beautiful, you know." Marcus ran his hand up her neck and jaw again. "So very beautiful. I believe you would make a striking queen."

She turned her head away, but the king brought her face toward his again. Leaning over, he kissed the girl, claiming before the multitude that he would one day make her his.

The crowd roared—the girl's own father the loudest.

She flinched but did not move as Marcus deepened the kiss. When he was through, he flamboyantly stepped forward, his arms swept out toward the throng, their cheers deafening.

The girl stepped back into his shadow. Her whole body quaked.

Rumple had never seen anyone look so petrified in all his life.

When her father came and captured the girl in a big bear hug, Rumple could just make out the tears streaming down her cheeks. To anyone else, they could be construed as happy tears, tears of relief and joy. However, he could tell they were anything but.

Marcus shooed her off the stage as quickly as she was brought up. He said a few more words to the people, but Rumple watched as the guards collected the girl and forced her into the castle— her father bellowing out her embellished achievements behind them the whole way.

He waited until the coast was clear before hobbling back into the servants' entrance. He wound through the back passageways, bursting into the bustling kitchen as they were preparing for the king's luncheon. Sliding along the wall so as not to be in anybody's way, he swiftly dipped down into the small cellar—his home.

Rumplestiltskin rummaged and searched through every single thing he owned, desperately trying to find the stones he had collected by the pond all those years ago. The last time he had even looked at them was on his sixteenth birthday. Tilly was convinced the pretty rocks had magical abilities and would one day help him. She was positive that because they had been in his pocket at the time of the transformation, they held a special enchantment.

After years of trying to make the striped stones correct his body, Rumple had given up. There was no doubt the pebbles had some sort of zing to them, some sort of mystical ability. Hadn't they shifted his clothing around the room and created a few moments of ease and happiness for him when the chores seemed too hard to bear? Before he gained as much strength as he had now, Rumple would constantly keep one of the stones with him to aid in carrying or moving something that would prove too heavy for him.

However, on his sixteenth birthday, after foolishly attempting to lift the ugly curse off his form yet again, his anger at the unhelpful rocks got the better of him. In frustration, Rumple threw the rocks across the room and vowed never to look upon them or hold them again.

Until now. He needed those silly stones now. If ever there was a time to find use for such enchanted things, it was right at this moment!

Tossing items about, he frantically searched through it all. Where would Tilly have put them? Where were they? He knew she would not leave them on the ground to be forgotten. She would have picked them up and placed them somewhere—somewhere safe.

His eyes roamed around the small room, his mind reaching as far back as he could remember to grasp anything—any little wisp of a clue as to where the stones could be.

That girl needed a miracle, and though he was not sure his stones could do all she required to keep her father alive, at least it would be a start. Heaven knew she needed some sort of hope to grasp on to.

Slumping onto his bed, Rumple laid his crooked back down and thought. One arm came to rest behind his head as he took a moment to sort through all those memories of Tilly to connect with one that could help him.

He was an incredible problem solver; he just needed a few minutes of peace to allow the puzzle to sort itself out in his brain. Closing his eyes, he sifted through hundreds upon hundreds of the greatest memories of Tilly, allowing his mind to find something—some clue to where she would have hidden what she considered to be his utmost treasure.

After several minutes, his eyes flew open. The windows. She had always said how the windows in his room would one day open to reveal his future.

He looked at the makeshift curtains and landscape paintings that had long ago become some of his dearest friends. Slowly, he got off the bed and approached the window closest to him. Raising the only hand that would reach that high, he felt all along the top of the frame and down its sides. He skimmed the curtains as well. But it wasn't until he lifted the pictures completely off their nails and flipped them over that he found the stones tucked between the frames and canvases—three stones in one canvas and three in the other.

Strangely enough, the blue-and-black striped rocks seemed to glow as brightly and as beautifully as he remembered when he very first found them. His long, crooked fingers tightened their hold briefly around the removed stones and their brightness increased.

Maybe they contained more magic than he imagined. Perhaps his window, in an odd sort of way, did open—creating a means to assist others, allowing him to be a part of this world and truly contribute.

CHAPTER FIVE

AUBRYNN SAT ALONE IN the large, richly decorated room, waiting for someone to remember she was there. The guards had silenced her father and sent him home quite a while ago. It was a good thing they removed him from the castle before he could create even more havoc for them both.

What in the world was she going to do? Had anyone ever heard of such an impossible thing—spinning straw into gold? What in the world was he thinking? Where had he gotten such a foolish, stupid idea from, and how would she be able to protect him this time?

She leaned forward and covered her face with her hands, reminding herself to breathe. In her anxiety, she often overlooked the simple act of inhaling and would make herself sick because of it. It did no good to expire on the sofa. She needed to breathe, needed to think her way out of this mess.

But what in the world was she to do? If King Marcus knew her father had appeared before him drunk and had lied, he would surely hang them both. Already the king had his suspicions—she knew he did, or he would not have put such a ridiculous ultimatum upon her.

And to marry her! Marry her? Was he out of his greedy wits? The man must surely be mad to want to wed a simple village maiden in return for such a nonsensical gift.

Oh, great heavens! How would she ever accomplish such a thing? She needed a miracle. Her shoulders shook and her head began to bob as the silent sobs washed over her again. Why? Why must life and her fate be this difficult?

This was impossible!

Her sobs broke with an unexpected wail. Instantly, she straightened her features on a trembling lungful of air. It would not do to be seen or heard sobbing.

No, she could not become hysterical. Not now.

To lose all hope now would be a waste of the years and years she had held it together since Mother and Rulayne died. There had to be a way out of this muddle. There had to be. But, heaven help her, she knew not what it was.

Aubrynn's shoulders shook again and a tear began to make its way down her cheek. How she despised her father! How she pitied and loathed the insufferable man! How she loved her father, the only true family she had. How she needed him to see her—to love her, to become a man she could be proud of— grateful for. And yet, it would never happen. She knew that now. Her foolish parent would always be the child she was never allowed to be.

She would forever be an object to him. Something to use and step upon.

Aubrynn rose in a flurry of muddied petticoats and worn skirts to seek a distraction from her horrid, worrisome thoughts. She needed something kind to look at, something hopeful. Her nerve-racked gaze flew around the large, cream-colored room, barely taking in the ornate furnishings, chandeliers, and paintings.

Her eyes skimmed one particular painting twice before she realized it was of the king. So distraught, so overcome was she that she failed to notice another person in the room with her until it was too late.

Aubrynn screamed at the sight of the fearsome, twisted man. "Who are you? What are you doing here?"

Rumple knew he should have announced his presence sooner, but was not sure how to go about doing so. She was clearly as distraught as he imagined she would be, and he did not want to alarm her more. He took a gentle, rolling step toward the girl, one hand out to ease her. "Shh, please, do not shout." To be caught talking to her could ruin everything.

"Who are you?" she asked again, quieter, taking a step back.

"I live here. It is all right. I do not wish you harm." He took another pace and was pleased to see that she did not step back this time. "I am here to help you, if you will let me."

"I am sorry. You startled me."

"Yes, well . . ." Rumple grinned a lopsided grin and continued, "I do have that effect on people."

Her eyebrows flew straight to her hairline and she attempted not to chuckle. "But where did you come from? I did not see you come through the door."

He waggled his brow and waved his arm about, chanting in a singsong voice, "It is because I am a magical being who can poof anywhere he wishes."

She grinned and shook her head. "No."

"You do not believe me? Oh-ho! Now what shall we do?" He took another rolling step forward. "Do I need to prove my powers to you, then?"

Aubrynn did not know why she felt like giggling as a schoolgirl all of a sudden, but this strange man very much made her do just that. "Yes. Yes, you must poof away from me this instant."

"Very well." He stood as straight as he could, which was only a few inches taller than her due to his crooked spine. "But I would have you close your eyes for a few moments, please."

"What?" Aubrynn bit her lip, her mirth obvious. "Is that not cheating?"

"Never!" He tried to assume the air of one who had been affronted. "I, perchance, do not wish you to know all of my secrets just yet."

44

She laughed. "But to ask me to close my eyes before you poof from existence is really rather telling, is it not?"

"Of course it is!" He grinned, his brilliant gray-blue eyes sparkling at her. "But again, poofing is an illusion I wish to keep unknown for some time. If not, it will not do to teach a maiden how to poof and find her in all sorts of hidden places throughout the castle? No, no. It is a long family secret and one I must vow to keep forever. So close your eyes, please, so that we may continue."

She tilted her head, not afraid of him one bit. "Are you always this strange?"

"Always." He attempted to mimic her and tilted his head too. "Are you always this difficult and argumentative?"

"I—" Her jaw dropped open. "No, actually, I am not."

"Good." He chuckled. "Then I see I bring out the worst in you. My job here is done." And with that, he flung a long line of shimmery fabric before her and poofed right before her eyes. He was gone.

"But wait!" she called out quietly. "Where did you go? You cannot leave yet!"

"Why?"

He was back! She spun around to the voice behind her. No, it was the king. Startled, she lowered into a hasty curtsy.

"Who were you speaking to just now?" he asked, his gaze searching behind her.

She almost told him, almost, but his frown checked her. "A mouse," she lied.

"A mouse?" One dark eyebrow rose.

"Yes. I—I was speaking to a mouse. I was trying to catch it, but it scurried away before I could."

His dark blue eyes raked over her features as Aubrynn held her breath, waiting.

"I do not know what game you are attempting to play, girl, but I would kindly ask that you remember I am not a king to be tampered with."

Aubrynn lowered her lashes and curtsied again. "Yes, Your Majesty."

"Look at me."

She obeyed and he stepped forward, his eyes connecting with hers. "You must look at me when I am in the room. Do you understand?"

She nodded, her eyes never leaving his.

His face softened for a second and he said, "You really do have the most exquisite face I have ever seen. Truly, you are remarkably beautiful."

Aubrynn flushed and was about to look away, but remembered at the last moment not to. "Thank you," she murmured, not sure what to say. No one had ever told her such things before.

"I do not particularly like brown eyes overly much—my own being as superior as they are. However, yours do have a bit of spark to them, a life all their own, something that draws me to look deeper." He stepped forward again, almost touching her.

Aubrynn was quick to move back.

The king's brows lowered, clearly upset. "Why must you be so complicated? Come here."

She took another step backwards, bumping into a small end table. "What will you do?"

"My word! You are frightened of me!" He laughed. "The small bird cannot even stand being in the same room as me."

She moved around the table, trying to put something between them.

"I am King Marcus, maiden. I am your king, your protector. You have no need to be frightened of me."

"Unless you deem it necessary to chop off my head."

"Well, yes, there is that." He took another step toward her. "Now come here and stop acting like a child. Do you know how many women would love to be alone in a room with their king?"

She had no idea what was coming over her, but apparently, she did not value her life as much as she had hoped when she answered, "I am not like most women."

CHAPTER SIX

KING MARCUS BARKED OUT a quick laugh of disapproval before swiftly walking forward and grabbing her arm, his face looming over hers. "Maiden, you will not be so forward in my castle. Ever. Do you understand me?" He did not wait for an answer before he continued, "You are here because of the graciousness of my heart. But mark my words, if you two are playing a hoax to get me to accept you as my bride, I will have you both destroyed."

She flinched, her eyes never wavering from his as he continued to hiss out his threats.

"You may have full confidence that you can bamboozle me with your trickery, but, my fair girl, you are quite decidedly wrong. I find it amusing, this claim that you can spin straw into gold. Why, it is simply preposterous! If you could do such a thing, why is your father not wealthier? Why am I just now hearing of this?

"No! I believe you cannot do such a thing—but I will humor you both this once. I will see tonight if you truly are the gifted sorceress he believes you are! I am wise enough to see that with someone like you within my grasp, I could control anything—make my enemies truly suffer! So, if you are capable of the impossible, I will guarantee you the crown upon your pretty little head. If you are not, may the demons of Hades rest within your soul, for I will make you pay for creating a mockery of me!"

He pushed her forcefully from him. Aubrynn barely caught herself from stumbling to the floor.

"Guards!" he shouted. "Guards!"

Uniformed men immediately began to pour into the room.

"Take this woman up to the tower I have instructed to be prepared for her and lock her inside! Block the door and see that no one goes in or out of that room until I come to visit in the morning."

"Yes, Your Majesty." The men bowed and collected Aubrynn. Without a word, she let herself be pulled along, the wall of men surrounding her. Her heart beat nearly twice as fast as usual as they marched rapidly up several flights of stairs. Their holds were tight, but not painful, at least. However, she had to catch herself to guarantee she would not trip.

As the corridors tightened and a spiral staircase presented itself, the men shifted their marching, allowing a few to lead the group, one to hold her, and several to follow behind. They rounded the last corner at the top of the tower shaft and hastily unlocked the large wooden door, the only room visible in the small stone walkway.

Thankfully, they stepped aside as she squeezed past, allowing her to walk into the room without being manhandled. She barely saw several piles of straw before the leader, the oldest of the group, began to speak, and she turned toward him.

"You should find everything you need. Unfortunately, we will not be able to assist you further once this door is closed." He paused a moment. His eyes gentled a bit as he searched her face. She was not sure what he found there, but whatever it was, a great look of pity came upon his features. "We wish you well, miss."

"I—thank you," she answered, longing to beg him to stay so she would not be alone.

"Please, do as the king asks, for your sake. Do everything he says."

How? It was impossible! It was all a lie! She wanted to shout and cry at the same time, but instead nodded her head and answered, "I will try. Thank you again."

The guard glanced at the other men, shaking his head slightly before looking past Aubrynn to the room. Great sorrow creased upon his brow as he frowned slightly. She could not imagine what he was thinking, but by the way his eyes searched hers again, she had to wonder if he had a daughter or granddaughter about her age. He must have known as she did that there was no way in all of eternity she would be able to do as her father claimed she could. Upon impulse, Aubrynn rushed forward and threw her arms about his shoulders. The guard held still for a bit and then surprisingly hugged her back.

"Do not worry for me," she whispered into his medallioned chest. "I will be fine. You will see."

"Hrrumph!" another of the soldiers coughed, causing her to pull out of the man's arms.

"Forgive me. I know you must go and do as the king commands. I will be well. You may leave me." She stepped back and watched the door close. The older guard did not meet her eyes again. With a thud, the room reverberated as the metal lock clunked into place.

Aubrynn stared at the closed door for a long time. Her hands wove themselves into the large, curved iron handle. She stepped forward and placed her forehead upon the worn, cold wood. Her life was over, or it would be shortly. Very, very shortly.

With a ragged sigh, she finally gave in to the deep sobs she had hidden for so long. Her shoulders heaved as she held on to the handle for balance, for purpose, to remind herself she was truly where she was—that this was, indeed, her reality.

This morning, preparing for the visit to the castle, seemed months and months ago—almost a lifetime compared to where she found herself currently. It was incredible to see how quickly her life could change through the actions of others.

Aubrynn wept.

Oh, how she wept. She finally allowed the sorrows of the deaths of her mother and sister to wash over her. Their illnesses and loss were greater than anything she had known at the time. And now, for certain she would watch her father perish as well, for on the morrow, the king would undoubtedly command his guards—perhaps even the exact same men who brought her here—to kill him.

Her knees buckled. She fell to the floor, still clasping the iron handle tightly with both hands, and sobbed against the door. The world she had tried so hard to hold together, the world she desperately needed to stay firm, began dissolving into slivers and threads beneath her. She was drowning in despair and she understood fully the meaning of hopelessness and defeat—for though she was brave to the onlooker, her world was simply and quite truthfully over.

She had nothing left to live for.

She could not save her mother or sister, and now to feel the weight of the foolishness of her father was beyond her. Life was done.

And she never truly got to experience or taste any of it. Always, always searching and reaching out for another who needed her more. Always fixing and righting every wrong.

Now this one she could not fix.

Her father would go too. He had to, because she was all out of life and wisdom and help herself.

It was done.

Finally, she released her hold when her hands began to go numb. Instinctively, she curled up on the smooth stone floor near the door and wept herself to sleep—tears forming a puddle under her cheek. Her final evening of life upon the earth was spent bitterly agonizing over all those she could not save.

Aubrynn had come to her end.

CHAPTER SEVEN

IT WAS A COUPLE of distressingly long hours before Rumplestiltskin could find a way to get to her again. Too many people about, too many servants using the old passageways, to be comfortable being seen heading up the tower to her room. He had nearly been caught by Marcus earlier when he was talking to the girl. He had heard his boot tread just in time to escape through the passageway before the king walked through the door.

Against the other side of the wall in the passage, Rumple had listened to all Marcus said to her, especially the threats. How he had wanted to throttle his brother! To speak to a woman like that, to treat someone with such force was unlawful in this country, and yet, Marcus continuously did so—not concerned about anyone but himself, believing he was more superior than the law—that *he* was the law.

Marcus was the one who deserved to burn in Hades, not the poor girl.

But Rumple had checked his temper and withstood the temptation to do what he wished to his brother. It would do neither him nor the girl any good to be caught in the king's wrath. He was more use to her here, capable of helping her.

But, oh, the pain she must be facing at the moment! How her mind must be plagued with confusion, knowing her father betrayed her. Rumple worried greatly for her.

Once the coast was clear, Rumple began his climb up the opposite side of the dark stairwell as rapidly as he could. The circular wall of the tower in reality held two spiraling staircases. The main one was about three feet wide and wound its way up with sconces and leaded windows overlooking the land and village roundabout. The other one was tucked within the small shaft that ran up the middle of the stairs. This one was for the servants' use, yet Rumple was not sure anyone knew or remembered it existed since he had never seen anyone else use it. The inner staircase was tight and extremely dark, but made the perfect hiding spot when the whole castle was commanded to search for him when he was a child.

Within minutes, he was able to push against the hidden wall and walk into the secret entrance of the tower. He quickly took in the dim room, lit only by the moonlight streaming through a leaded window—the piles of hay were nearly five feet high all across the side wall. He glanced toward a makeshift bed, a small mattress and blankets—she was not there.

Searching the room, his eyes peered into the shadows for the girl. She had to be here. "Hello," he whispered softly as he crept forward. "Maiden, where are you? I have come to help."

Rumple bumped into a large wooden object and it took a few moments to determine it was a spinning wheel. He was confused briefly until he remembered her father had said she could spin straw into gold. Shaking his head, he ran one hand over the thing. How could anyone be so foolish as to tell such falsehoods to a man as ruthless as his brother? Had her father no common sense at all?

He moved away from the cumbersome spinning wheel and ran his hand along the wall until he found the small fireplace. Quickly, he knelt before it and stirred the ashes to life using an iron prong nearby. Once the sparks began to fly and produce some light, he easily found the firewood stack and placed a couple of logs upon the embers.

They caught soon enough and cheerfully blazed their warmth into the dingy room. As he turned, pleased with his accomplishments, Rumple's heart stopped at the sight of the beautiful girl curled up on the ground, the glow of the fire dancing upon her dress and arms and worried, sorrowful features.

Her small frame moved up and down as she slept. Her thick lashes could not conceal the tear stains or swollen eyes, but she was relaxed and slumbering now.

A deep ache settled within his chest as he truly realized the predicament this girl had found herself in. How horrid it would be to fall asleep believing you were completely alone and there was no help for you.

Rumple hunched down, his leg twisted awkwardly beside him, but he did not come closer to her. He did not want to disturb the fragile sleep she had exhaustedly reached. Instead, he looked again around the room and took in the great work ahead of him. The piles of hay were thick and plentiful, and somehow, some way, he had to find a technique to turn it all into gold before sunrise. He shook his head once more and rubbed his weary eyes with his twisted fingers. He could do this. He had to do this. He just had to figure out how.

First things first. He plopped himself against the closest wall and grabbed a few fallen strands of straw from the ground. Then he fished in his pocket and pulled out a stone. Concentrating with both hands—one grasping the straw, the other the stone—he made several attempts to work the small rock into doing as he wished.

After a full wasted hour, he could make the pebble levitate the hay and even move it about, tying it into many different shapes. He could even make the hay glow, but he could not for the life of him figure out a way to spin it into gold.

How did one go about doing such a thing? Chanting did not work, mind power did absolutely nothing, and even wishing was completely useless. Frustrated, Rumple stood and walked over to a particularly large pile of hay. Tilly had always believed these stones would change his life—always. And though he wished that could be so, he did not see how it might be possible—how anything truly worthwhile could be possible with such simple rocks. He leaned against the straw and lowered his head, tilting it to one side. The prickly pieces did much to wake him up and stimulate his muddled brain. He needed an answer. There was something missing—but what?

When his eyes settled upon the spinning wheel, it took him a minute to fully comprehend what he was seeing.

Of course! He stood up.

She must *spin* the straw into gold.

Anxious and too afraid to be overly hopeful, he grabbed a good-sized handful of straw and moved over to the spindle. Sitting down, he set one leg out before him and used the other one to balance the straw. Then he put the stone in his mouth and fumbled with the string of the spindle, placing a few strands of straw on it. He began to slowly spin the wheel, allowing the string to wind through it, and concentrated with all of his might that the straw would spin into gold thread.

He could barely make out a faint glow of blue from his mouth and knew the rock was working. He was just trying to keep the wheel spinning and the slippery straw from falling off the string onto the floor instead of turning onto the spindle. His crooked fingers were not as much use as he wished them to be.

After several attempts to keep the straw moving up the string with one hand and the spindle whirling with the other, he was finally about to slip one of the smaller strands in. His thumb had to rest against the string to get the support he needed to keep the straw on. He remembered to concentrate on the stone at the last possible moment as the straw was moving through. Instead of turning into gold thread like he hoped it would, the strand stayed the same shape and fluttered, spiraling to the floor. He glanced down and kicked it with his foot. Obviously by the way it fluttered, it was still hay. Sighing, he bent down and picked the thing up. It was heavier than he expected.

Slowly he turned it over. One half of the piece was hay, but the other half had come out solid gold and glistening. Huzzah! He had done it! The straw was gold. The straw was gold!

With a relieved gasp, he choked on a bit of emotion, the rock falling from his lips onto his lap. He could not fully believe his eyes. He had done the impossible. He could save her after all.

Overcome, Rumple held his face with his crooked hands, wiping the wetness from his eyes. Oh, he honestly had not believed he could do it. Thank the heavens he could. Oh, thank the heavens!

The girl moaned and stirred from her spot a few feet from him. She turned slightly, the back of her head toward him. And then she sat up, staring at the happily flickering fireplace.

CHAPTER EIGHT

AUBRYNN BLINKED AT THE fireplace cozily dancing before her. How did she get a fire in this room? Moving a bit, she glanced down at where she had been lying upon the cold stone floor. Her dress was crumpled and wrinkled around her. She had clearly fallen asleep on the ground and had never moved from the doorway. Looking to the right, she beheld the large pile of straw waiting for her to turn it into gold. She groaned and turned farther still to see a small bed with blankets and the like.

"Before you twist completely around and see me, I had better warn you I am here this time."

Aubrynn jumped at the sound of his voice and screeched when she turned more fully and saw the strange man in her room. "Goodness! Do you intend on frightening me out of my wits every single time I am alone?"

He smiled. "Well, not every single time. Maybe a few more, though, yes." He moved his leg as he sat at the wheel. "I did warn you I had that effect on people, did I not?"

"You most certainly did." She grinned, grateful not to find herself alone. "But how did you get here? Who are you? And what in the world would make you come and be here with me now?"

He leaned back and folded his arms as best he could. "One question at a time. And I promise I will answer them all for you—anything you want to know, I will gladly answer. But first, I am famished. Do you have any food, perchance?"

"I—" She blinked again. "I—I do not know. Wait. Stop. Just for a moment. Can we at least begin with one thing before I try to figure out what has happened to the knapsack I brought with me to the memorial earlier—just a moment, please?" She knelt to be at eye level with him and brushed her dress out as best she could before stating, "I am Aubrynn Sloat. I know it is not proper for a girl to introduce herself first, but as you can see, I am with a man without manners who clearly does not know these things, so I must make do."

Rumple threw his head back and laughed a great hearty laugh. "You have caught me, my dear. You are correct. I am something of a savage with no real manners, as you can see." He bowed his head in acknowledgement. "Thank you for putting me rightfully in my place at such a time like this. You, Aubrynn, may call me Rumplestiltskin."

"Rumplestiltskin?" Her brow furrowed slightly. "Rumplestiltskin? What name is that? Do you have a distinct heritage? I have never heard of it before."

"Or Rumple, if you would prefer something easier."

"Is that truly your name?"

"Do you see someone else who would fit it more than me? Yes. It is what I am most usually called."

"But why? I do not understand"

"I have never had a person so vehemently dismiss my name before; I do not know quite what to make of it. Do you perhaps not see how rumpled and stilted my skin is? Should I stand for you then?" He made as if to get up.

"No. Please stay seated." She stood, however, and approached him. "Forgive me if I have come off discourteously just now. I did not mean to. It is just—were you always this way, or has something happened?"

His eyes locked with hers. "Does it matter?"

She read layers of hurt within his depths and realized this was indeed a very sensitive subject, but no matter how painful it was, it meant something to him that she was curious enough to ask. "Yes, it does matter."

He stared at her a full two minutes before simply stating quietly, "No."

"You were not born this way?"

"No, I was not."

"What happened?"

He glanced away, his gaze taking in everything at once without looking at her. "A curse. And that is all I will say about it."

"No, please, do not close the subject off now." Aubrynn stepped forward and clasped one of his hands. She was surprised to feel the zing of awareness that pinged through her at the simple touch. For a second, her whole arm felt tingly and alive.

When his eyes met hers, she could tell he was as shocked as she was. He could feel it too.

A bit flustered, she rushed out, "What were you called before the . . . uh . . . the accident?"

"Curse. It was a curse."

"Very well. What were you called before the curse?"

She held her breath as he took in all of her features, much as the king had. She wondered for a small moment if he too thought she was beautiful. He was obviously weighing his answer as she implored him with her looks to reveal his secrets. However, he grinned and shook his head, bringing a bit of easiness back into their exchange. "It does not matter what my name was then, does it? All that matters is who I am now. And I am most definitely nothing but a Rumplestiltskin."

She took a deep breath, abdicating the conversation to him. There was no reason to push the issue further. "Well, hello there, Rumple. I am very pleased to meet you." She withdrew her hand and immediately took his up again to shake.

WHEN HE TURNED HER wrist within his hand and brought it quite properly up to his lips, she giggled, her eyes sparkling mischievously down at him. "Thank you for asking, though," he said. "I do appreciate the gesture."

He watched as a spark of something flicked across her face, but then she smiled again and answered, "You are most welcome."

"Now, may we partake of some food?" He chuckled at her look. "I only ask because I assume you are more famished than I. Knowing the king as I do, he has probably neglected to send you up some nourishment, and if we are going to be awake all night spinning this straw into gold, we will most definitely need something to keep our vigor going strong."

"I . . . uh . . . you . . . ?"

"Yes?"

"Halt! I cannot follow this train of thought quite so quickly. Can you step back a pace or two and tell me again about spinning straw into gold? You say we will be doing it?"

"Well, of course! That is why I am here, is it not?"

She choked. "Is—is it?"

"Well, that is why I came."

"Truly?" She grasped his hand tighter. "You are not jesting?"

"No. I am quite purposely here to help you, my lady."

She brought his hand up to her mouth, her shoulders shaking greatly as she processed all he was saying. Aubrynn's eyes darted back and forth between his as she asked, "You honestly can do this? You—you can change straw into gold?"

"Yes. It took me some time, but I finally figured out how while you were sleep—"

She quickly embraced him and kissed him quite soundly upon the lips.

It was not quite the kiss Rumple had always imagined experiencing with a beautiful maiden—especially with her sobbing, incoherent mutterings and salty tears, but who was he to complain?

Without another thought, he wrapped his arms tightly around the girl and kissed her back. He was not sure when another such opportunity would arise, and so, of course, decided it was best to make the most of it.

And sob Aubrynn did. Great, heaving sobs upon the poor man's mouth, neck, chest, and mouth again. "Thank you," she muttered at the end. "Thank you. Just thank you, so very, very much." She pulled back a bit and wiped her eyes with the sleeve of her dress and her fingertips, his arms still holding her tight. "How will I ever thank you?"

"Ahem." A couple of surprise laughs burst forth from him before he stated, "I think you already have."

Embarrassed and a bit disconcerted, she broke from his hold completely. "I am sorry. It seems all I will be saying to you is how sorry I am. But I am terribly sorry for accosting you just now. I do not know what came over me. Honestly, I am a much calmer person—not prone to such emotional outbursts and behavior."

"Yes, so you have told me before. However, I do find it hard to believe."

Aubrynn flushed. "Please do not tease me. I am sorry to behave as I did."

He schooled his features. "Do not be. I certainly am most enlivened by your—uh—enthusiasm for life. Your distinct zest and eagerness is refreshing and definitely anything but boring."

She leaned down, collected a pile of straw from the floor, and tossed it at him. "You are not a gentleman."

He grinned. "I know. I am a savage, remember?"

"I do not believe I will ever be able to forget." Her smile matched his.

"Good. So, may we eat now?"

Aubrynn laughed. He looked so much like a little boy, with his twinkling eyes and silly grin. There was no help for it. She simply had to laugh.

CHAPTER NINE

AUBRYNN STOKED THE FIRE, placing another log on top and churning it to bring more light into the room while Rumple went downstairs to raid the kitchens and find something for them to eat. He promised he did it all the time and that the cook was used to him foraging for food, and would most likely have something set aside for him.

She bit her lip as she prodded the logs a tad more. He really was quite remarkable in his concern for her. What man would have thought she would be hungry? Who would have cared or remembered her the way he did? And how did he come to be here now? Out of all the times she needed a savior most, he suddenly appeared.

He must be an angel, something divine and not quite real, for who else would have thought of her before their own needs? She knew her own father would never have done such a thing. Frankly, she had never known of a man who was as gentle and genuine as this Rumplestiltskin seemed to be. He could very easily have come after he had some supper of his own, but he did not— waiting first to see if she needed something.

Her heart warmed. She folded her arms and stepped away from the fire, her eyes taking in the stark room. What would she have done without him? Looking upon the spinning wheel, she walked over to the old instrument and sat down where he had been. Could he truly turn straw into gold? Her gaze fell to the odd piece of straw at her feet—half gold, half straw.

Oh, my word. He did it!

Quickly, she fetched the thing up and twirled it about between her fingers, trying to remember what he said about attempting to create this article before she kissed him. Something about it being many tries before he was successful . . . perhaps.

She looked up, her eyes focusing on nothing particular. How long had he been attempting the impossible? How long had he sat here trying to achieve her feat for her? Who would do such a thing? Who would work for hours helping someone else—involving themselves with someone else's deeds and finding a solution for them? Who would concern themselves over such things?

After a minute of silence, it dawned on her.

Me. She sat straighter upon the small stool. *Me. I would. But is there really someone else out there who loves as I do? Who cares about people and life and who risks their own to help someone else? Someone besides me?*

Her heart began to glow. Quite perfectly and happily within its chest, it glowed and beat and lived and breathed.

Who was this man? Who was he honestly?

She knew he wished her to think of him as rumpled and stilted, but how could she? Yes, he was crippled—distinctively so. And his features were distorted to a point, but not too badly.

Were they? He was not so ugly that he could not be considered beautiful. He sincerely was beautiful. His smile, his wit, his friendliness and ease, his laughter—they all exuded such beauty. How could one look at him and not think him wonderful?

She had only known him a few hours, but he was perchance the greatest friend and ally she had ever made.

He was an angel. She knew it. He had to be. So perfect and divine and—and well, perfect.

Needing to do something, Aubrynn stood up and set the golden straw upon the seat and then looked around the room. Seeing an old broom leaning against the wall near the bed, she collected the thing and began to sweep up the bits of fallen hay. Clearing the floor and tidying up the room allowed her to feel productive. He had said they would be spinning the straw as soon as they had eaten, so she took it upon herself to collect a pile and set it close to the spinning wheel, which would allow the work to go faster. Unsure exactly what she would be expected to do, she wanted him to know she would help him as best she could and be of any assistance he needed.

Soon after another small sweep of the newly fallen hay, Rumple walked in through the hidden doorway. His arms were bundled full of goodies. She quickly set the broom against the wall and helped him into the room.

"How did you carry this all up those stairs?" she asked, glancing down at his hobbled foot.

He smirked boyishly. "I have magical powers, remember?"

Aubrynn rolled her eyes as she removed one of the heavy loads from his arms. "Does this magic power include lightening bundles?"

"Actually, it does."

"Oh." She was surprised. "Well, that must be helpful."

He grunted as he set the rest of the load upon the ground. "You have no idea, especially on days like this." Lowering himself to the floor, he gingerly moved his leg out of the way. "So, we are in luck, my fair maiden."

"We are?" She was quick to join him, settling her skirts upon the newly swept ground.

"Yes. It seems the kitchen staff was anticipating your meal, so there were extra things lying about for you."

She smiled as he unwrapped and removed a few peeled, boiled eggs, two different cheeses, muffins, some cold ham, a large chunk of bread, two apples, a peach, dried nuts, and several tarts. "My goodness! This is a meal fit for a king! How will we be able to eat half this much food?"

He grinned and bit into a boiled egg. "That is the beauty of it. We do not have to eat this all—now we have something to break our fast, too."

His gray-blue eyes danced in the firelight as he chewed, quite proud of himself. Aubrynn did not hesitate to slice some cheese with a small knife he had revealed and began to nibble upon it. As the delicious cheese made its way down her throat, she realized how completely famished she was.

"You are an angel!" she exclaimed as she bit into a chunk of newly broken bread, her hand quickly finding an apple. "How did you know I would be this hungry? I did not even know I was this hungry."

He shrugged and then answered around a mouthful of ham, "Just an inkling I had."

"You will, mayhap, forget my manners for a moment as I catch up to my appetite?" She grinned, her own mouth full of apple.

"Of course!" He chuckled. "As you can see, my savageness has come out as well. So, let us be merry beasts together."

Gratefully, Aubrynn tucked in quite a bit more than she believed she would be able to. However, with a fully happy tummy, she was more than willing to get to work. Rumple dusted off his hands and began to help her tuck everything away for later. Once it was all stored nicely upon her bed, he sat down at the spinning wheel again, removing the golden straw from the seat first.

"This is a bit troublesome on my own, so I am hoping you could help feed the straw into the spindle itself. See? Like this." He picked up a few pieces of hay from the pile she had next to the stool and began to spin the large wheel. She watched the way he held the straw in place on the string, feeding it slowly into the needle.

"Is that all there is to it, then?" she asked. "Just threading it onto the needle?"

"Not quite." He spun the wheel a final push and the straw wove through, but came out looking the exact same way it had before. She tried to catch it before it fluttered to the floor, but to no avail.

"So, what is the trick?"

"Magic. I have to do the magic with this little thing, or nothing will happen." He pulled out a beautiful blue-and-black striped rock. "I will need help spinning and working the straw into the spindle, since I must hold on to my stone and concentrate somehow to create the gold."

"So that is your secret—a little rock."

"Yes." He waggled his eyebrows. "Now you know everything."

"Not quite."

"Close enough. At least you know the most important parts. Well, are you ready to spin some straw into gold?"

"Yes!"

CHAPTER TEN

IT TOOK SEVERAL TRIES with both
of them working together to eventually
settle upon a system that would spin the
straw into gold. Aubrynn noticed quite
early on that he was right. As long as he
did the spinning of the wheel and she fed
the straw in, the magic would work. He
had to be concentrating on the actual
spinning for it to transform the straw into
gold, so she would feed the straw on the
string as he continuously spun the wheel.

Once they became used to the task
and got a bit quicker, they saw that the
gold would come out in long strands and
curl itself upon the floor before hardening
into shape. It was still a very complicated

task, one Rumple, especially, would have to concentrate extremely well to attain.

Never before had he worked so hard for so many hours in a row to achieve the same outcome over and over again. It was tedious and difficult and worth every single smile Aubrynn gave him as their momentous miracle began to truly transform the room.

Every half an hour or so, Rumple would stop to stretch his limbs, and using the magic stone, he would lift the heavy gold off the floor and stack it in new piles where the hay had been against the wall.

One of the remarkable effects they noticed was that it would take approximately three or four pieces of straw to form the same size of gold. So the piece that he had initially made, they soon figured, must have been at least four times as long on the gold end as it was now. It did not matter, since it allowed them more room to walk about the place as they continued to alter the large piles of hay into smaller stacks of gold.

By sunrise, their unattainable task was nearly complete.

Both Rumple and Aubrynn had formed blisters upon their fingers—hers more so, due to the direct contact her knuckles and thumb had with the string, but his palm was quite worn with its consistent pushing of the wheel. They were cramped, emotionally and physically exhausted, but amazed at all they had accomplished.

There was just one smallish-sized pile of straw left, approximately to Aubrynn's knees, but she was simply too fatigued to even attempt getting it.

"Do you think the king will notice that little pile of hay when all the rest of the gold is gleaming before him?" she asked as she plopped down upon the floor. Her back ached from leaning over the spindle for all those hours.

"Aubrynn, are you well? Do you need to sit here, on the seat?" Rumple made to move, but as he stood, his right leg gave out on him. In a flash, he tumbled, sprawled crookedly facedown upon the floor next to her bed.

"Rumple!" She scrambled to kneel beside him. "Are you hurt?"

He groaned in response and slowly flipped himself over. "Mayhap. I will let you know later."

She half attempted to chuckle as she looked down at the wonderful man below her. "What happened? You were standing one moment, and the next—"

"And the next I was slumped upon the floor, looking the fool in front of a charming maiden."

"You are not a fool! My goodness, who does not stumble every now and then? We all do."

"Yes, well. Me more than most, I am certain." He attempted a grin.

Her eyes caught his; there was great pain within their depths. "Rumple, are you hurt? The fall must have damaged something. Your knee, perhaps? Your ankle?"

He shook his head, those eyes regaining their sparkle. "Look at you! The mother hen clucking about in great anxiety."

She gasped. "I am not a mother hen, and I do not cluck." Tucking her feet further under her, she moved closer, her arm going across his chest. "Though I do worry about you. Are you sure you are fine?"

"I will be shortly, as long as you stay next to me a few minutes more."

She looked up to the rafters before grinning down at him. "You are incorrigible. And you will not tell me what is wrong, will you?"

"Most likely not."

She worried her lip, her teeth tugging and pulling on it. "Why ever not? Should not someone know what ails you so they can be of assistance?"

"Do you know how beautiful you are?"

"No." She blushed. "And it will not do to change the subject."

"Why not?"

"Because you are in pain, that is why! And we simply do not need to be discussing my looks with you sprawled about on the floor in agony."

"But what if those looks dim the agony a bit and make me remember only how glorious it is to get to know such a maiden? Then is it proper to speak of your beauty?"

"Rumplestiltskin!"

"Yes, Mother Hen?"

She groaned and giggled and lay right down upon his chest. "You are hopeless."

He reached down and ran his hand through her long, soft, dark hair, and then said quietly, "So I have been told many times."

"Hmm," she muttered into his warm frame. His fingers caused ripples of explosions through her whole back. "I could fall asleep right here, this instant."

Though his back ached greatly from the extra pressure she caused, he could not think of anything more dear to him in all the world than a few minutes more spent with her sleeping upon his chest. "It was exhausting, but we did it."

She tilted her face to the side, loving the gentle feel of his hand. "You did it."

"We both did."

"Yes, but without you I would have . . . I would have . . . What would I have done without you?"

"Shh," he whispered. "I was here. I would not have left you alone anyway. I would have always come."

She turned and pressed a kiss upon his stiff shirt. "Thank you."

"You are most welcome." He sighed, his chest heaving up and carrying Aubrynn as he did so. "However, there is one small problem in all this."

"And what is that?"

"The king will be back any moment and he cannot find me here."

"Oh! You are right!" Aubrynn went to pull away, but his crooked fingers caught her and held her against him.

"Just a bit longer, please?"

She snuggled back down. "I am not hurting you, am I?"

"No," he lied. "Just give me a few seconds longer of humanity before I have to face the world again."

She grinned against his shirt. "Is that all you need, then? I can definitely provide that."

"Well, some humanity and maybe a kiss, too."

"What?"

"Yes, I think I most definitely need a kiss."

"Rumple!" She came up enough to see his mischievous eyes.

"What?" He blinked. "A man can dream, can he not?"

She flushed bright red. "Of course he can. I probably *could* give you a small token of my affection for all you have done for me." Goodness! What was she saying? She went even more red.

Rumple laughed. "Come here, you." He pulled her right up his chest to about an inch or so from his very handsome lips. "May I kiss you, my fair maiden? Just once more?"

All at once, Aubrynn forgot how to breathe or speak. "I, uh—" she croaked out. Clearing her throat, she tried again. "Uh, yes. Yes, you may."

In a sudden burst of seriousness, Rumple's smile dropped, his gaze taking in every millimeter of the amazing woman before him. She was truly beyond anything he could have ever imagined. Slowly, his hands wound themselves up to her neck and head and then carefully, as if she were the most delicate china, he brought her mouth to his.

Aubrynn sighed as his soft lips caressed her mouth, her lashes fluttering shut. Nothing had ever seemed so perfect before. His lips tugged and pulled and searched hers until she thought she would melt, sending a series of exciting sparkles throughout her whole form.

It was by far the most deliciously wonderful thing she had ever done.

And she never, ever wanted to stop.

"Aubrynn Sloat!" the voice bellowed beyond the door. "It is I, the king. Do I have permission to enter and see if you have achieved all that your father promised me you would? Am I a rich man soon to have a bride? Or will your father be hanged?"

CHAPTER ELEVEN

RUMPLE PULLED AWAY FROM her and then quickly came in for another swift kiss as she was attempting to scramble to her feet. "I do not wish to leave," he murmured against her mouth.

"Nor do I want you to go," she whispered back.

"Do you think he will go away if we are silent?"

She grinned. "You are completely impossible."

He kissed her cheek and then let her go, his eyes dancing before her. "Yes, I know."

The king pounded on the door this time. "Awake, maiden, and speak to me, or I will burst through this door."

"I am up, Your Majesty. A moment please to arrange myself," she called out.

"And that would be my cue," Rumple whispered. Holding out his hand, he allowed her to assist him to his feet. "Hand me the bundle of food and I will hide it here in the passageway for you."

She quickly did as he asked and fetched the striped stone too. The room was still a bit in shambles with straw littering the floor, but that could not be helped now. "Hurry, please. And be safe."

There was a distinct limp that was not there before as he hobbled over to the hidden door.

"You are hurt!" she cried as she followed him.

"Shh. I am fine. Just stiff." He silently cracked the panel of stone a bit and looked into her worried face. Such a heart she had, such a sweetness. His own heart beat wildly, and he promptly kissed her once more. "Good luck." He stepped through onto the stairs. Bouncing down a step or two, he placed the bundle next to the door.

"Thank you," she called as he closed her off into her own room again.

"Maiden!" The king was clearly an impatient man.

In her eagerness to allow the king in, Aubrynn did not have a moment to dread the prospect of him coming. Indeed, she was quite eager to show the miracle before her. She smiled. "You may come in now. I am ready."

Immediately, the large, clanking lock clicked and King Marcus was in the room, his eyes beholding the piles of gold. "You have done it!" he exclaimed in a hushed tone. "You, my dear, are simply wondrous!"

He walked over to the coiled piles and tried to lift one. It was simply too heavy without the magic stone. "My, they are real!" His hands caressed the gold lovingly, and he seemed a bit entranced by it all. "So beautiful. So perfect. So, so, so incredible!" He turned around and stared at the tired maiden before him. Sprigs of straw stuck out all over her. She looked worn and exhausted, but happy. Indeed, she should be happy! She had just secured herself a king for a husband.

"Do you know what this means, my dear Aubrynn?" He came forward and clasped her hands within his, not noticing the wince in her eyes as the blisters rubbed. "It means you and I will have a very prosperous life together."

She blinked, her brain too fuzzy and focused on the pain to fully comprehend all that he was saying. "So, you are happy then? You are well pleased?"

"Happy?" He barked out a laugh. "My dear maiden, you have made me much more than happy! I am exuberant! I am ecstatic! I am so well pleased with you, I mean to move you out of this room this very instant and do something simply divine with you! Something—something to reward you for your tremendous talents." Wildly, he picked her up and twirled her around.

"But wait!" She was a bit dizzy when he set her down again. "Can I not sleep first? Do you mind terribly if I slept for some hours before any such thanks are given?"

"Oh! Yes! You must sleep. You must. You must keep up your strength."

"Thank you."

The king let her go and walked back over to the gold—touching it again for several moments before saying, "This is simply not enough, though. We will most definitely need more."

"More?" Aubrynn's stomach dropped. "Truly? There is not enough there now?" Her fingers began to ache again.

"Oh, no!" He whirled around to look at her—then checked himself when he saw the girl's face. "You, we—how else will we be able to afford the type of wedding we hope to have? How will we be able to secure the castle from our enemies and see that it is fine and decorated in the greatest of fashion for those who wish to visit? Aubrynn! No! I am afraid we have only just begun!"

The girl collapsed on her bottom, right onto the stone floor. It was too much—she was too exhausted. Neither she nor Rumple would be able to do all he would require of her. She felt like weeping.

He rushed forward and knelt before her. "Aubrynn, you must see that this is the best way. You must."

She shook her head and covered her face with her sore hands. Her last thought in the world would be to do this all over again. She simply could not imagine it.

She felt the room shift before she heard him stand up. Instantly, the king's tone changed. "You will stop this nonsense and do as I have asked, and you will be grateful for it, too!"

She kept her head in her hands, not willing to risk his wrath more.

"Aubrynn Sloat, I command you to finish this. You will create all the gold this kingdom requires, or I will hang you! Do you understand me?"

When she did not move, he shouted, "Look at me!"

Slowly she removed her hands and looked up at his forceful features—her own glaring back at him. With great strength, she stood to her full height and placed her hands on her hips. "Then kill me now. I am done working for you. You are cruel and selfish and will only use this gold to better yourself—thinking nothing of your subjects. If this is what marriage to a king will be like—eternal, selfish slavery—then take your gold and destroy me! For I will not have it!"

He grabbed her arm, yanking her toward his face. "You will never speak to your king in such a way again, madam. I am not in the habit of being told what to do." He brought his hand up to strike her, but then changed his mind at the last moment. "Sleep here!" He thrust her away from him and toward the small bed.

"I was going to allow you to sleep in the one of the castle suites, but I can see you need to be reminded who your betters are. Guards!" he called out. "Guards, bring me the girl's father! Fetch him from the village and be prompt!"

She could hear the heavy footsteps of the guards making their way down the spiral staircase. "What will you do to him?" she asked.

The king smiled. "Everything I wish to do to you right this moment." He stepped forward, loving the way she scurried away from him and onto the bed. "You almost made me lose my temper with you and that would not do, would it?" He stopped and brought a hand up to inspect his ring. "No, my dear *queen*," he spoke softly down at the bright red stone, "you are about to make me a very rich man. And just think—when you do, I will love you forever."

She swallowed. "And if I refuse?"

His piercing blue eyes met hers as he raised one thick, dark eyebrow. "Then a hanging for your father will not be sufficient. I shall simply make him pay for your every crime and outburst and willful stubbornness. I will torture him, my dear."

She gasped.

"And if you are not careful, I shall make you watch, as well."

"You are evil! Pure evil!"

He raised a hand up in a cautionary gesture. "Careful, my dear. Your father is already going to receive several lashings as a result of this insolence. I suggest you mind your manners and be a good girl, or you will live to regret it."

Clenching her jaw, Aubrynn remained silent. Clasping her shaking hands together, she lowered her eyes and willed herself to remain calm. The blisters stung.

"Do we have an agreement?" he asked smoothly. "You will do all I ask, correct?"

"Yes," she muttered.

"Good. Rest, my little one, for in a few more hours, I shall have the servants remove this gold and bring up twice as much hay—to be completed on the morrow." He leaned down and pulled her hands from her lap. Inspecting them from side to side, his fingers lightly traced the blisters. "Tsk. Tsk. It is a great loss for royalty to lose their hands like this. However, they will be well enough soon. As long as you do as I ask." He pinched one large blister on her forefinger, causing the fluid to spill upon her hand and onto her lap. She did not flinch. "I wonder how many blisters I can produce on the Sloat family today. It will be a very interesting game to play, perhaps."

She kept her eyes lowered and remained silent.

"Good girl. You are learning. I can see that you and I will be friends again shortly. Enjoy your rest. You shall need it. I will be back again tomorrow."

And with that, he was gone.

CHAPTER TWELVE

AUBRYNN CURLED UP UPON the makeshift bed and covered herself with one of the blankets available. She was so very exhausted; she did not even allow her mind to wander toward all that was happening now. Instead, she focused on the great feeling of heaviness that came over her. Allowing her eyes to drift shut, she let out one sob of remorse and fatigue and fell directly to sleep.

She slept so deeply and for so long that Rumple began to be worried. The guards had already come in and changed the gold out, carrying each coil between three of them at once down the steps. Once they removed all the gold, they then came back with twice as much hay than before for her to transform.

After he awoke from his nap, Rumplestiltskin made his way into the kitchens to find out what he could of the girl and what Marcus had chosen to do. It took no time at all to apprehend from the servants that she had defied the king and was now asleep, awaiting another long night of spinning straw into gold.

As soon as he could, with another fresh round of supplies and water, he made his way up to the tower and knocked lightly upon the hidden door. When she did not answer, he peeked his head in and beheld the sleeping girl with the doubled mass of hay around her.

Quietly, he crept into the room, and sweeping off a small patch of ground, he began to artfully arrange the food on the blanket she was not using to welcome her when she awoke. Except she did not awake—not for at least two hours more.

Rumple had already begun to work on the straw by the time she started to stir. It was a long process, but he was able to make some progress with one of the piles in that time. It was better than allowing it to sit there and precious minutes to pass.

She stirred and stretched before she heard the sound of the wheel.

"Good morning, dear," he called around the pebble in his mouth. He was still upon the seat and did not look up until the straw was completely through, then he removed the stone and asked, "How did you sleep?"

"Like a baby." She grinned and stretched again, wiggling her toes. "And you are here."

"I am here."

How was he so wonderful? "Thank you."

"I would not miss it for the world."

She sat up, her eyes taking in the massive amount of straw. "Could he be any greedier?"

Rumple glanced over to the piles and sighed. "In my experience, I have never known any man to be quite like King Marcus, though his father did come pretty close."

"Have you lived here long, then?"

He nodded. "All my life."

"Being a servant of the castle is all you have ever known?"

"Most all of my memories revolve around serving the inhabitants of this castle, yes."

She pushed herself off the bed and walked over to him. "My! Look at all this food *and* the gold. You have done quite a bit."

He shook his head and snorted. "Not nearly an eighth of what I can do when you are helping."

She picked his hand up off the wheel and turned it over. "We do make an incredible force together, I must agree." Her fingers lightly traced his worn palm. "How bad is it?"

He shrugged. "I have felt worse." He flipped his hand and captured her fingers for inspection. He winced as he tilted them from side to side. "Aubrynn, what will we do with you? You cannot work in such a state. They will be a bloody mess within an hour or so."

She shrugged and tried to mimic him. "I have had worse."

His eyes flew to hers. "Truthfully?"

"No."

"Aubrynn, this is not right. Does the king know you have these blisters and are incapable of doing all he asks? I think he should be told."

"He knows."

"You are certain?"

She pulled her hand out of his and pointed to her finger. "Do you see this?"

"The one that has popped, yes."

"It was a present from the king."

Rumple captured that finger and pulled it to his mouth, kissing the redness.

She smiled as his gray-blue eyes caught hers over her hand. He really was completely adorable. Then she chuckled and whispered, "I have to relieve myself."

Rumple's whole body froze for a moment and then he threw his head back and laughed. "Of course you do! Who would not need to?"

"Um, so how does one go about doing so in the castle?"

"How bad is it?"

"Uh—pretty bad."

Rumple shook his head. The king was a fool. Clearly, he had not thought of such things as taking care of her basic needs. "I could take you down the secret stairs to a room designed for relief, if you would like? Or I could fetch a chamber pot for you, and I will leave the room and you can just toss it out the window? Which would you prefer?"

"Either, or . . . something. Soon." The idea of walking down all those stairs did not appeal, but neither did using a chamber pot and tossing it out the window, especially knowing Rumple would be back again soon. But honestly, if something was not taken care of shortly, a lot more embarrassing things would happen than the use of a silly bedpan.

Looking at her face and the way Aubrynn had begun to hop a bit, desperate times awaited. "How about we do this," he answered. "We will use the stone to glide you down the stairs quickly and silently to where we need to go, and then I will be sure to bring a bedpan up for future use. Yes?"

"Um, fine. That will do. But could we hurry, please?"

Standing, Rumple clutched the rock and, while concentrating, he watched it glow. He wrapped one arm around her waist, holding her tightly next to him, and then grinned as they began to float off the ground. He concentrated on the door opening before them and then slid her down the long, spiraling passageway.

By the time they had gotten to the end, she was clinging to him for dear life. It was brilliant to feel her so close.

He slowly opened the door and peeked out. As soon as the coast was clear, he rushed her to the back end of the castle, dodging down old, deserted passageways the whole time. She gasped and clutched his shirt as the magic worked faster and they were transported quicker than he had ever experienced before. During the complete duration, he concentrated solely on reaching the room unnoticed. The magic worked and kept them completely shielded from being seen.

Rumple smiled. These rocks were definitely more useful than he had ever thought possible. "We are here!" he said as he lowered them both gently down.

"That was quite possibly the most enchanting and fun thing I have ever done in my life!" she exclaimed. "I was terrified to squeal or screech or anything, in case we were heard, but oh, how I wished to do just that! We were flying. I cannot believe it, but we were truly flying!"

"Pretty glorious, is it not?" He pulled away from her and pushed her gently toward the room. "If you walk inside, you will see a large ledge and a hole. You may use it. There is also a towel and soap and water to wash yourself with after you are through."

"Oh, goodness! This is a luxury indeed. How wonderful."

He chuckled. "I will close the door to give you some privacy. Please hurry."

Aubrynn returned to him rather quickly with the biggest smile upon her face. "Do you have any idea how marvelous you are? Just how simply, perfectly superb it is to know another human being like you?"

He was leaning up against the wall. "It is because I can fly, is it not?"

"Well . . ." She grinned.

He pushed off from the wall and chuckled. "I knew it." Holding his arm out, he waited.

Aubrynn giggled and stepped into that waiting arm, her hands going around his shoulders and grabbing a handful of his shirt, her face just mere inches from his.

Rumple's eyes explored her happy features a moment. What would it be like to wake up each morning to such pleasing looks before him? Such a contented glow and warmth about her he had rarely seen in anyone else. Tilly had come close, but she still did not have the spark that Aubrynn did. Gently, he leaned forward and tasted her lips again.

She sighed and held on tighter to his shirt.

For a moment he had completely forgotten where he was and that he was with the castle prisoner, but when sounds of the kitchens began to make way to his ears, he immediately pulled back. He knew several servants would pass this way shortly on their way up to the dining room. As swiftly as possible, he concentrated on the stone and lifting them up.

"Why did you stop?" she whispered near his ear.

Her voice triggered a series of shivers through his neck and shoulder. They hovered slightly before dipping. "Hush. You will make me lose concentration."

"But I liked kissing you."

"Shh!" He pulled them back up and they began to move forward, nearing the first of the passageways.

She grinned and lowered her voice, turning directly to the shell of his ear. "Can you kiss me as we fly?"

He nearly dropped them both that time. "Maiden!"

She chuckled and tucked her head into his shoulder. "I will behave now."

Rumple's silent laugh could be felt throughout his whole chest.

Could there be a more perfect man in the world?

Honestly?

Aubrynn giggled and snuggled closer as they flew back to her waiting room.

CHAPTER THIRTEEN

IT WAS SEVERAL MINUTES after Rumplestiltskin and Aubrynn had eaten and while they were again preparing for another long night of spinning straw into gold that Rumple surprised Aubrynn, as she was placing another pile of straw next to the spinning wheel, by capturing her palm and wrapping a long, narrow strip of fabric around it.

"Where did you acquire such a thing?" she asked, fascinated with how well he managed to wrap the strip around her hand and then each finger and back around her palm again.

"I tore it from one of the blankets." He looped the loose end and tied it off, securing it to one of the other straps around her hand. Once done, he repeated the process again with her other fingers.

She inspected his handiwork all around and then smiled. "Thank you. I believe you may have saved me."

Rumple grinned and leaned crookedly upon the spinning wheel. "So, when you are queen, will I be granted knight status?"

"If I am ever queen, you will be given the grandest chamber in this house—mark my words!"

His smile fell. Slowly his eyes took in her every feature. If things were different, it would be he who would be marrying her soon. His heart began to thump quite strangely and hollowly within his chest.

Aubrynn took a step closer. "What? What is it?" Her cloth-covered hands reached up and held his arms. "What have I said to bring such a look upon your face?"

He shook his head slightly to chase the silliness away. "'Tis nothing."

She tugged on his sleeves, her eyes searching his. "Falsehoods do not become you, my dear. Have I said or done something that has triggered such an awful memory to show itself upon your features? Rumplestiltskin, I promise, whatever it is—whatever I have said—I did not mean to harm you further than you have obviously been harmed. You, you of all the people in the world do not deserve such treatment from me; especially after all you have done—"

"Hush." He placed a finger upon her soft lips to silence her. "You have done nothing wrong. It is life that has intruded upon my thoughts, nothing more." His thumb gently brushed against her bottom lip.

"Kiss me," she said against his hand.

He chuckled. "You are intent on surprising me at every turn, are you not?" His fingers splayed across her jaw as his thumb continued to caress her mouth.

"Rumplestiltskin, kiss me now, you fool."

His serious eyes met hers. "I am a fool. I am a fool for wanting to be here the longer I am with you. I imagine soon, I shall never want to leave you."

"What?" Confusion marred her sweet features. "Will you leave me soon? Please do not leave me. What would I do without you?"

"Shh." He brought his mouth down to capture hers, kissing her tenderly. "I would never leave you. Can you not see I am completely bound to you? Just as this magic has woven and transformed straw into gold, so has your heart woven and transformed mine to forever be changed and bound to yours."

She inhaled swiftly and pulled back, her lips forming a perfect O of astonishment. "No one has ever said words such as this to me."

"No?"

"No. No one has ever thought to do so."

"Well, that is a shame."

"Rumple, why would you say them?"

He glanced over her features again and smiled ruefully. "Because they are true."

Her breathing began to come in great gasps as she tried to process all he was telling her. "But they cannot be. Not wholly."

"And why is that?"

"Because, because . . ." She looked down at her dirty dress and held it out to him. "Well, look at me! I am just a girl who lives in the village. And you are a servant of the *castle*!"

Rumple laughed and glanced down at himself. "Have you not noticed that I am not much to look at, my dear?" he asked, amazed she seemed to disregard his stilted body altogether.

"Why? What do you mean?" She seemed genuinely confused.

"Aubrynn, sweetheart, I am a crippled man who has been cursed to remain this way forever. No beautiful young woman in her right mind would wish to come within three feet of me."

"Yet, you cannot keep me away." She grinned and stepped toward him.

He foolishly wrapped an arm around her. "And why is that?" His own heart paused to hear her response.

"Because I do not see what you see. I cannot. Your true self has shone too brightly, despite your crippled casing. You are simply too marvelous, too good to be considered anything that resembles a curse." She cuddled up closer to his chest and wrapped her arms around his bowed back.

Rumple let out a long-awaited sigh at her answer. A great feeling of warmth settled over his heart, kissing it and then slowly winding its way through his limbs all the way to the tip of his hair. His whole being filled with the glorious enchantment of her words. Never had he believed a woman such as she would enter his life—never did he even dream it would be possible. He tried desperately to make her see reason—to make them both see reason, though he was too delightfully warm to say much more than, "But it will not last, this goodness you feel that I am."

"Of course it will," she mumbled into his shirt.

He tried again. "But what occurs when this is all over? What happens when all the straw is spun into gold— then what?"

"Then my father lives and the king is happy and does not try to hurt us."

"What else, darling?"

She pulled just far enough away to look at him. "There is more?"

"Yes. Think. What else happens?" Just knowing she did not fully grasp what was coming in her future made him even more entranced by her. What female would not jump at the chance of becoming queen, to wear such costly apparel and live in such a rich way? And yet, she did not see it. It was not even a part of her thought process. But he must

118

make her see. She must prepare herself for her future—a future without him. "Once the gold is all created, and the king comes to claim his prize—what happens then?"

Aubrynn gasped. Her eyes locked with his. She shook her head, not willing to accept her fate. "No."

Slowly and steadily, Rumple nodded. "Yes."

She stepped away and looked around the room, still shaking her head. "No, no."

"It is the way of things. It is what must happen."

"Can we not just end this now? Not turn anything else into gold and halt what has already begun?"

He stepped toward her, but she fell back a few paces. "No, we cannot. King Marcus knows it is possible; he will stop at nothing now to guarantee you provide more gold for him. Your father would surely die."

"But I do not wish to marry him!" she cried out. "I do not want any of this! I do not need gold or anything to make me happy! Do you think he will just accept the gold and let me be?"

"And lose his only means of making more? I highly doubt it."

"But it is not me—it is you."

"Covering for you, to protect you."

She turned away and walked over to the largest of the stacks of hay. Leaning against the prickly surface, she shut her eyes and rubbed her lips together and willed herself not to cry.

When Rumple made his way over to her, she would not meet his eyes. Instead, she looked down and muttered, "He is cruel. He is heartless and cold and a mockery of all that this kingdom could be—all that it would be if . . . if . . ."

"If what?" he asked, gently, his hand coming up to brush a stray strand of hair away.

She looked up and straightened a bit. "Do you ever wonder what would have happened if the little prince had not died?"

Rumple flinched but did not speak.

"If he had not left us all—do you not wonder if he would have perhaps been a different king? Kinder, more loving, more caring?"

"I think about it every single day of my life."

Her eyes snapped to his. "And?"

"No. I do not think he would have been a better king. In fact, I worry he would have been worse."

CHAPTER FOURTEEN

CONFUSED AND TORN, AUBRYNN pushed away from the hay. "Why would you say that? How do you truly know how he would have turned out?"

"I knew his father well enough. I was here as I watched the man raise King Marcus; it was not appealing. He taught the young boy to be ruthless and spoilt and selfish. He would have taught . . . Freder—er, the other son to be the same."

"Frederico. I know the prince's name was Frederico." She smiled. "Everyone knows it. It is no secret."

"Yes, I know."

"Then why do you hide and stumble upon it as if it were?"

"No reason. I would prefer not to disrespect the dead, of course."

She raised her eyebrows and tilted her head to the side. "You have an issue with names, do you not?"

"Definitely not." He grabbed a pile of hay and moved over to the spinning wheel to set it upon the mound there.

"Then why will you not tell me yours?" She collected a pile as well and brought it over. "I have been going mad trying to sort it through my mind and figure out this great mystery."

"Have you now?"

"Yes. But I am no closer to solving the puzzle of your name as I am to coming up with a reason as to why you would hide it from me."

"Honestly, it is best to leave well enough alone. The more you know, the deeper trouble you may find yourself in," he answered cryptically.

"Rumple." She sighed. "You are hopeless."

"As you have mentioned before."

"You do apprehend that the more elusive you become, the more determined I am to solve the riddle of your name, correct?"

"I do know that I probably have offered to help one of the busiest busybodies in all the kingdom, yes."

Her jaw dropped. How dare he say such a thing of her? She was most definitely not a busybody—certainly not anything like the other women of the village. "Why, you little . . ." Aubrynn dipped down and grabbed a large handful of the straw and tossed it all over him.

Rumple sputtered and spattered at the hay as it stuck in great chunks from head to toe.

"I am not a busybody. Retract that statement at once."

He grinned and shook his head. Portions of straw fluttered their way upon the floor all around his feet. "Forgive me. I believe I may have confused my wording. You are most likely not the busybody I had once thought you."

"I would think not! Thank you."

"You are indeed more of a monstrous menace!"

Needless to say, it was some time before the two of them stopped tossing hay about the place—giggling incessantly—and began to actually spin the stuff into gold. But once they got to work, they toiled swiftly and efficiently.

Rumple made sure her hand was re-covered with a fresh strip of fabric before they began, since it had come loose in the straw-tossing contest. Amazingly, the bandage ended up allowing them to work even more rapidly than the night before.

Even though there was a much greater multitude of the hay than previously, her fresh bandaging allowed the straw to grip easier and her fingers to feed it into the string with better tension. The chore went so well that they were actually finished a good hour or two before sunrise. However, they were not any less sore for their troubles, and fatigue had settled upon them both greatly.

Rumple sat upon the floor, his back against the bed as he partook of the last of the apples.

Aubrynn, too tired to even contemplate eating, gathered her skirts about her and sat down alongside him.

He held one arm out and she quickly nuzzled her head into his chest, wrapping her hands about his waist for stability. He leisurely began to trail his fingers over her hair and back as she listened to the crunch-crunch sounds of the apple being eaten.

She loved the way his chest rose and fell slightly with each action. And the way it was all so real and natural and perfect and easy to be next to him like this.

She closed her eyes for a moment and sighed contentedly. The ticklish trails of pixie dust floating along her back and hair from his fingertips were all she could fully concentrate on.

When Rumple adjusted himself slightly to toss the core of the apple into the makeshift knapsack, she kept her eyes closed and held on tighter. Once he had settled again, she fell into the simple rise and fall of his breathing and the sanctuary she felt near him.

He wrapped his other arm around her as well, to keep her safe. After a few minutes, he tried to tug one of her hands forward to inspect them for blisters, but she grumbled against his shirt and so he let her be, just content to listen to the sweet sound of her breathing and take pleasure in the tenderness she provided to his aching bones.

Tonight proved to be equivalent to the day before. It was not comfortable for him to hold her, but it was worth the inconvenience it caused to have her so

126

very close to his heart. Soon, her breathing became more spaced out and her hold became just that bit more heavy and serene.

"Aubrynn," he whispered against her brow. "Aubrynn, are you asleep?"

She stirred slightly, but there was no answer.

He grinned tiredly at those dark lashes as they brushed her beautiful cheeks. "I love you," he murmured. When she did not respond, he continued softly—his heart warming at the admission, "I love you more than I ever thought possible to love a human being." He waited again, when there was no reply he said, "It is true. No one has treated me as an equal before, other than Tilly. But you do even more than she did. She loved me, but was still somewhat scared of me and felt indubitably sorry for me."

He waited a moment more, his lips brushing her forehead again. "Yet you, you do not feel those things overly much. You will still quarrel with me and toss hay at me and snuggle right against me as if I were someone special in your life, as if I were someone you could love forever." He stared off at the spindle a moment and then over to the large, gleaming piles of gold twice as high as yesterday before kissing her brow again.

"Oh, Aubrynn, do you have any idea how much you have brightened my life these past couple of days? How you have truly enlightened my soul and allowed me to see the world so much more beautifully? Your heart is the epitome of everything good, my dear. It is you. You think it is me, but no—I know better. I am not half as good as you are. Would I have cared for you the same if our roles were reversed? I am afraid not. And I know of no one who would have acted as you have done. For no other woman would have seen me as you do, all full of scars and twisted as I am, and seen past this shell and treated me as you do. You are goodness divine. And I will always love you."

He closed his eyes and continued to whisper, "No matter what happens tomorrow, no matter where this road takes us both, I will be your ally forever. And I will move heaven and earth to come to your aid whenever you require it."

Looking down at her arms encircling him, he grinned before kissing her brow tenderly again. "Oh, how I would have loved to have raised a child with you and held that dear son or daughter and chased them and cuddled them and loved them as you have taught me. Oh, how I would have loved all of that, but, my dear, I do not believe it will be so. I do not see how it can be. I am not allowed the happiness you are, my sweet." He paused a moment before taking a deep, silent breath. "I will never be allowed it. For you will never truly be mine.

"Sleep on, little one, sleep on until morning, for I fear it will be my last night with you eternally, and I would rather have this once more to remember with the aches and pains that will accompany such actions than a lifetime of remorse for not holding you when I had the opportunity. So sleep, angel, sleep. I am here to hold you and provide you the strength to face the morrow."

His shoulders began to shake. He could not speak another word, but could only think the last of it all.

I love you. A thousand times I love you. You possess every inch of my heart. And I thank you, dear maiden, I thank you for everything.

CHAPTER FIFTEEN

THE POUNDING ON THE door woke Aubrynn with a start.

"Aubrynn Sloat, are you awake yet? I have come to collect my gold," came the shout of the king.

Clearly, he was not a happy being this early in the morning. She looked out the window. It was still dark—the sun had not even come up yet!

Rumple stirred within her arms as she responded, "Forgive me, Your Majesty. I have just awakened. Please allow me a moment to myself and I will permit you to enter shortly."

"So, King Marcus has come to interrupt our slumber and collect his gold," Rumple muttered beside her.

"Yes, it would seem so." She pulled away and smiled sleepily at the lovely, crooked man beside her. Silently, she leaned forward and placed a kiss upon his cheek and whispered, "Thank you for holding me and allowing me to use you as a pillow."

His hand snaked up and captured her chin, his mouth finding hers in a perfectly delectable good-morning kiss.

"Hmm." She sighed before kissing him one last time and pulling back.

He watched her lazily before stretching and then stifling a groan. He was so very stiff. "You are welcome to my chest anytime you wish to use me." He yawned and stretched again.

She ran her hand over the bowed front of his shirt while he stretched. "Are you certain it does not harm you to have me sleeping like that?"

"Do you not believe I would tell you if you were hurting me?"

She climbed to her feet, her taut legs protesting. "Yes," she whispered, "it seems exactly like something you would do—never mentioning the fact that I am most likely killing you."

"Killing me? My goodness!" He attempted to raise himself up off the ground, but his elbows and shoulders and hands would not cooperate. With a thud, he crashed back down. He moaned and exhaled, eager to let out an expletive of some sort, but held his tongue in her presence.

"Rumple!" She rushed forward, forgetting for a moment to be quiet. "Are you hurt?"

"What did you say?" bellowed the king. "May I come in now?"

"Just a moment more," she quickly answered, her eyes meeting Rumple's.

Already the lock began to click.

"No!" Aubrynn shouted. She hurried to the door and blocked it. "Sir, I have not finished dressing. Please allow me the courtesy of some more time."

"You have one minute more and then I am coming in," came the terse reply. "I do not appreciate having to wait."

"Yes, Your Majesty." Aubrynn waved at Rumple to get up, but he was clearly stuck. His legs were so stiff, his joints had failed him. "I am hurrying as fast as I can," she called back for good measure.

"I believe I will—I will need some help," said Rumple.

"Certainly. I am here." She came around to his shoulders and, pulling from behind, attempted to heave and push him into standing position. "Let us do this quickly now."

"My legs are so sore, the joints will not allow for much give this morning." He attempted to use his arms again to lift himself, but yet again they failed him. "I am sorry, my dear."

"Shh, it is fine."

She grunted and lifted with all her might.

Rumple regained his footing from the sheer grit and determination of Aubrynn's will. "You did it!" He awkwardly lunged forward, his hands balancing himself on the spinning wheel. "I do—I do not feel so well." His breathing became extremely labored all of a sudden.

"Use your stone!" she hissed. "What have you done with it? Let me get it for you so you may fly out of here. It is obviously too painful to walk." She glanced about the room and then back at him. "Where have you—?"

Pain clearly laced his features. His arms were trembling so much, she was afraid he would slip from his hold upon the wooden spinning wheel. His mouth began to take on a life of its own as he began to choke and gasp before her.

"Rumple? What can I do? What do you need? Tell me!" she whispered.

All at once, his legs began to quiver too.

"No, no, no." She held on to his waist. "Hold steady, my dear, hold steady a moment longer."

Rumple lunged forward.

Aubrynn's throat tightened as she watched him lose all control and collapse to the ground again. She was only able to catch one arm before it struck him in the face, but could not stop the rest of him from falling. "Rumple, what is happening?" She knelt before his quivering form, lugging him onto his back. "What is it?"

His eyes were gone from her—staring up at the ceiling for moments and then gone completely from view. They rolled around while he stuttered and jittered about. It was quite positively the most frightening thing she had ever witnessed before. "Rumplestiltskin!" she hissed. "What can I do? Tell me, please! Come back to me!" She leaned over to capture his shuddering face between her palms. "What is it? Do not leave me now, whatever has happened. Please do not leave me now!"

"Your time is up, maiden!" barked the king. "I am coming in."

Aubrynn's eyes lighted upon the small, striped stone that jiggled loose from Rumple's pocket. There it was! The lock to the door clicked loudly again. Grasping the stone tight, she fell forward across his trembling form and, closing her eyes, wished with all her might.

"Take us away from here. Please take us to safety, small stone. Save him, please, please save him."

The little rock began to glow near her face, and Aubrynn slowly opened one eye to stare in amazement at its beauty. She had done it! It was working.

She heard the door swing wildly against the inner wall before she felt the stale breeze hit them both.

Rumple's chokes and gasps grew louder with each shake and spasm.

"Please, please take us to safety! Take us to safety now!"

"What in the world is he doing here?" bellowed the king.

Flash.

They were gone.

CHAPTER SIXTEEN

AUBRYNN HELD ONTO HIM as they whizzed through a tunnel of long streams of light and color. The motion of them zooming through the air almost covered his convulsions—almost. They dipped down, and she squeezed her eyes shut and felt the air shift as they collapsed onto something that, while not hard, was not very soft either. Whatever it was, she could feel it had a fabric covering.

Rumple continued to jolt and shake before her as she climbed off him. She could barely see a thing in the darkened space. It was cold, and though there were muted sounds in the distance, she felt decidedly alone and very safe from the king, though not from Rumple's terrifying ailment.

What should she do? Was he truly dying before her? How could she help him?

She saw the stone glow again within her hand and then experienced an overwhelming sense of peace come over her, as if it were trying to tell her that all would be well soon.

She took in a deep breath of air and willed her heart to slow down. The worst was over—he would be well.

When his gasps and chokes began to sound more like gurgles, she brushed aside the foam that had begun to build around the corners of his mouth. Tugging him to his side and allowing his face to fall forward, she reached around the area where they were and collected a small blanket. Using it, she wiped his face clean and held him as best she could.

"Rumple, can you hear me?" she asked him, her eyes slowly adjusting to the darkened room. It was most definitely a room of some sort. "Can you hear me, dear?"

He shook and quaked for a minute or two more before peacefully coming to a stop.

She held her breath, afraid to believe it was over. Placing the back of her hand near his nose, she felt his intake and outtake of breath. Heaving a sigh of relief, she lay down next to him, her arm holding tightly to his. When she followed the dark shadows of his neck and face, she was surprised to see him staring at her.

"Well, hello there. You are back." She smiled.

Rumple glanced over her face and pursed his lips together.

"How do you feel?" she asked.

"Mortified." His eyes closed as he muttered, "I am sorry. I should have warned you I could go into such convulsions, but I did not think to do so."

"You startled me."

"I am positive I did do just that." He brought a hand up to her elbow and clasped it, their arms crossing over the other. "Are you well? And can you ever look at me the same again?"

"The same as what?" She blinked, shaking her head slightly. "Yes, yes, I—I am fine, as long as you are. I was so afraid you were dying there for a moment."

"I know. I heard you."

"Oh, Rumple." She scooted in a bit closer, her eyes making out his dark orbs and long lashes in the darkness. "Please do not leave me." She frowned, trying desperately to hold in her emotions. "I was so afraid—so, so afraid I was losing you."

"Now, do not, my dear." He came in closer to kiss the bridge of her nose. "I am well, as you can see. It is something that happens from time to time, just a few minutes of quaking, but all is well."

She sighed as his warm breath eased over her cheeks, sending a million sparkles skittering along her neck and back.

His lips skimmed down and kissed the tip of her nose. "I am more worried you will never wish to have anything to do with me now that you have seen me as such."

"Such as what?" She pulled back slightly to make out what she could of his features.

"Well, me at my worst, of course."

"There are some moments when you speak of yourself that I am quite certain if you say one more word I may throttle you."

He slowly grinned, his dark eyes sparkling. "Has anyone ever told you how wonderful you are? And how much you make a man wish he could be throttled by you?"

"Rumple, stop distracting me and listen." She clutched his arm tighter. "You are a crippled man, yes, but that does not mean you do not breathe and think and see and laugh and care the same as everyone else. I do not regard what ailments are imprisoned within your shell. They are not who you are—it may be your trial, but you are not defined by this outer casing. You are glorious. You are magnificent. And I cannot—I simply cannot—lose you. So, will you kindly warn me if there are any more disorders I should be aware of, and how to properly attend to them when they do happen?"

"I love you."

She gasped. "What? What did you say?"

He sat up slowly, his eyes going around the dark room, and then he smiled as if he knew the place. Pulling her up to a sitting position as well, he held one hand within his and leaned over and whispered near her ear, "I love you."

Heat and goodness exploded down her neck and pinged to her shoulder. "Say it again," she whispered. She smiled when he inhaled sharply, loving the effect she had on him.

"I love you, Aubrynn Sloat. I love you as a man loves a woman."

Twisting around and tucking herself right into the crook of his chest and neck, she asked, "Why? How is this possible? How is such an angel ever to fall in love with me? *Me*—of all people?"

"Because, as I told you a few hours ago while you were snoozing on my chest, I feel you are the one who should be exalted. It is your goodness, your ability to see me when no one else does—you who are more precious than anything. It is you I could not help but fall in love with."

She closed her eyes, a smile plastered across her face as she processed all he was telling her. "Rumple?"

"Hmm?" He wrapped his arm around her tighter.

"Do you think you will ever ask me to marry you?"

He balked. His whole body went rigid. "You wish me to ask you for your hand?"

"I—is that a bad thing? Should I not wish or wonder what it would be like to be yours forever?"

His heart sped at a pace he had never known it to beat before. "Aubrynn, do you have any idea what you are saying? And to whom you are saying it?"

She pulled back and looked him square in the eye. "Rumplestiltskin, if this has something to do with the fact that you are a crippled man and I should not look at you in such a fashion, can I please throttle you now and be done with this whole mess?"

He chuckled. "Yes. Do your worst. I cannot believe what I am hearing. Is that so hard to imagine, that I would be truly questioning—"

"Questioning my sanity. I know! And it vexes me to no end."

"I love you."

She pushed against his shoulder. "Do not try to distract me again with your great declarations. I have not responded in kind, if you notice, and I likely never will if you keep pestering me with your nonsense of never believing I could be enchanted by you."

"So, you are saying you are enchanted by me?"

She opened her mouth and then closed it. "Possibly." She rolled her eyes and nudged him with her shoulder this time, much softer. "Possibly, but you already know this, or I would not be sitting in this darkened place with you, worrying if I will lose you." She looked around again, trying to make out the murky shadows. "Just where are we?"

"Do you not know?"

"How would I?"

"What did you think of when you worked my magic rock? It will take you wherever you envision when you use it," " he said, and then continued before she could answer, "Well done with that, I must say! Truly genius, the way you figured out the stone so quickly. I was sure I would be lying there on that floor, expiring away, when the king walked in."

"You were."

"Yes, but you charmed us away before he could see me."

"He did see you. Did you not hear him?"

Rumple clasped her hand. "You are sure—quite positive—that he saw me? And recognized me?"

"I was positive at the time, yes. I know he saw someone, but it would seem he definitely was familiar with you." She looked in his eyes. "Why? Is there something else I do not realize besides the absolute notion that he did not know his servant was helping him? Is there something else—something that is causing you to sit up as straight as that?"

"This is my room."

"Your room?" She shook her head. "You do not get to distract me again."

"I live in the cellar under the kitchen."

She paused and stared at him. "You do not have a bed in the servants' quarters?"

"No."

"You live here, under the kitchen?"

"Yes."

"Why?"

"Because I am hiding."

"You are not a servant?"

"Not wholly, no."

"Then who are you?"

CHAPTER SEVENTEEN

RUMPLE MOVED BACK AND got off the bed. He hobbled over to collect his flint and then lit the oil lamps about the room one by one until the whole place shone brightly.

Aubrynn smiled when she beheld the cozy chamber full of vibrant reds, golds, blues, and browns. Even the tattered rugs had once been quite magnificent and were rather colorful. Her eyes fell upon the richly woven fabrics encasing the landscape paintings. "I love the imaginary windows! What a clever idea."

"Yes. I enjoy them as well. Though, I cannot take credit for the scheme. One of the maids, when I was quite young, created them for me."

"One of the maids? She has helped you?"

"Yes, she essentially designed this whole room. It is because of her that I was able to stay here so long and remain unseen. She cared for me as a mother would have."

Aubrynn scooted off the bed and walked to his makeshift dresser. It had a large fabric layer of some kind, perhaps an old scarf that covered the whole top of it. Her hands lightly skimmed the wooden toys he had neatly stacked upon the fabric. "How old were you when you first came here? You must have been very young."

"I was five."

She glanced over several different objects—miniature paintings, paperweights, shells, feathers, books, drawings, ornaments, all sorts of odds and ends—his treasures, all nicely displayed and cared for. "Was that around the same time your accident happened? The one that crippled you?"

"It was no accident."

Her eyes flew to his across the room. He was standing next to an old crate with a small silver tray upon it. "What do you mean? Someone did this to you?"

"I was cursed, remember?"

149

She waited for him to say more, but when he did not, she walked toward him, her feet treading upon the worn carpet. "Who are you?" she asked again. "You were too young to have suddenly gone into hiding. No mother would have just tossed you aside. Who are you?"

He looked away, his eyes settling upon the brightly polished tray near his hand. One finger slowly started to trace the thin etchings within it. "You would be surprised at what a mother could do to a cursed child."

Aubrynn touched his shoulder. "But, Rumple, she did not—she did not really. No mother would have . . ."

He closed his eyes and turned further away from her.

She clenched her mouth and blinked back a few sudden tears. Her hand started to caress his shoulder. She could hardly ask the words that she knew she must, "Rumple, were you truly cast aside when this happened to you?" She sniffed and blinked more tears. "My dear, were they frightened of you? And terrified of the curse?"

Blank, dull gray eyes turned and met hers. "It was worse."

No. She shook her head. No. "How could it be worse than that? You were a small boy! A young, frightened little boy, were you not?"

He pushed away from the crate and walked over to the bed.

She followed but stayed a pace from him. "Rumple, how scary and horrid for you—how alone you must have felt! And now you say it was worse? What could have made it worse than this? To be cast aside to live alone at such a young, young age!"

"They announced my death."

She froze. "I beg your pardon?"

He leaned over and picked up a pillow, slamming it into the old wooden headboard. "They told everyone I died."

"Your family threw you—a child of five years of age—out of their home and announced to everyone their son had died?"

"Essentially, yes."

"And a sweet maid felt sorry for you and took you into the castle and raised you and cared for you as a mother would?"

He sat down, his hands rubbing his face briefly, wiping moisture from his eyes. "Yes, Tilly—Tilly loved me. I am so very, very blessed to have had such a brave soul in my life. She was the only one who treated me as though I deserved to live, as if I were not a monster."

Aubrynn's heart soared. Oh, how she would gladly wrap her arms around such a woman and thank her. "Where is she? Which one of the maids is she?"

Rumple inhaled and then slowly let out his breath before answering, "Tilly died last year from illness. It will be a year to the date of her death in about three weeks' time."

She slowly lowered herself next to him. Taking his hand in hers, she whispered, "I am so sorry. You have had it very rough, have you not?"

He shrugged and smirked, his eyebrows dancing at bit before he took in her serious gaze and then answered, "Until you came along."

She leaned forward, captured his jaw, and kissed him delicately upon the lips. "I love you."

Rumple's shoulders began to shake slightly.

Alarmed, she stood quickly up. "Is it happening again? Are you beginning to quake?"

"No." He sputtered out a few short chuckles. "No, my dear, I am trying to a great extent not to cry and look a fool right now. And I must be failing miserably and looking quite dim if you believe me to be having convulsions."

"But why?"

"I have waited years to hear those words, and never believed I would." He took a deep breath, calming his soul. "And here you are, so lovely, so brilliant—sitting in the room of a cursed boy who is unwanted by everyone left on this earth—and you tell me that you love me. I must shake for a bit. The emotions are too strong to suppress fully. It is impossible. All of this is impossible to imagine."

She touched his shoulder.

Capturing her hand, he brushed the worn bandage away and kissed her palm. His blue-gray eyes looked up and seared hers. "Thank you."

She smiled as he kissed her palm again. "For?"

"For loving me, of course."

She took her own deep breath, not sure whether to throttle him for his silliness like she had promised or kiss him again. Instead she asked, "What is your name?"

"Rumplestilts—"

"Your real name."

He let her hand go and stood up. "You know I cannot tell you that."

"Why?"

"Because if you knew, the king would surely kill you."

She stood. "Be rational. He would not surely kill me. He believes I can turn straw into gold."

He threw an arm out. "Do you hear him now? Do you hear the guards plundering the castle looking for us? Or marching outside tearing the village apart brick by brick to find us?"

She paused. "No."

He stepped forward, trying to make her see reason. Collecting both of her hands in his, his gaze bore into hers. "King Marcus has been trained to be extremely intelligent, to look for the unseen—to be ruthless. He is waiting. He is piecing it together and waiting."

"You believe he knows it is you who helped me?" she asked.

"He knows of me, though he has not looked overly hard for me. He knows I exist within this castle, and he knows I am cursed—which translates to some as having use of magical entities. I believe he has—if not yet, he will shortly piece it all together, yes. Especially if you are correct and he did indeed recognize me."

"Which in short, means . . . ?"

"Once he ascertains that it is me who has helped you, you become obsolete and worthless to him. As long as he is still partially convinced you are of merit to him, he will keep you."

"And by knowing your real name, this will convince him to kill me?"

"Yes."

"But why? How does that fit into your reasoning? It makes no sense."

"You must trust me, my little one. There is much that does not make sense, I know, but for reasons beyond what you can imagine, you would be annihilated if he knew you were acquainted with my name. You would be the first one he would destroy—gold or no gold. It would be too much of a risk to keep you around."

"But—"

"I only brought up the gold to remind you not to feel too powerful in this castle, as all may change swiftly. As I believe it may be doing now."

Frustrated, she pulled her hands away from him. "I do not like it. I do not like any of it."

Rumple grinned ruefully. "Yes, well, it is the way of things."

"What do we do now? How do we survive this?"

He shook his head. "I do not know. But we will."

Brown eyes locked with striking blue gray. She nodded. "We will." She took another deep breath and then grinned, attempting to lighten the mood. One eyebrow rose jauntily. "And when we do, I shall know your real name."

Rumple rolled his eyes and tried to tamper down a grin. "Rumplestiltskin, maiden. That is my name. It is the only name you will ever know me as. Do you comprehend why?"

She stepped forward, her hands playing with his shirt across his chest. "Of course. It is because you love me and wish to keep me yours forever."

"Good."

"But it is more fun to imagine knowing your real name. I will figure it out eventually, mark my words."

He groaned.

CHAPTER EIGHTEEN

KING MARCUS PACED WITHIN his royal chambers, his great boots clomp-clomp-clomping upon the stone ground. In this particular spot, he preferred to keep it barren of rugs or carpets or the like. He enjoyed the therapeutic steadying sound of his leather heels as they hit the floor again and again.

Frederico had been helping the girl!

He knew it was impossible for her to achieve such a ridiculous thing all on her own. He stomped two more paces and then spun abruptly on his heel to return the way he had come. He needed a plan of action. Something to ferret them out—something to guarantee that his brother suffered as much as possible.

The horror Frederico had caused this family! The pain they had been put through because of his interactions with that witch! Living with this scandalous secret was too much. It was time his wretched brother died.

He paused, his boots sliding to a simple halt. The girl would have to die as well. She would. It was obvious she knew who Frederico was or she would not have allowed him near her. She would not have been protecting him and lying upon him as she was. He sneered. It was disgusting to see them in such a fashion, her head over his bent chest like that!

No, Frederico must be planning some sort of revolt with the girl—something to put himself back on the throne. And that would not do. Oh, no, Marcus had worked too hard to build this kingdom up after their father died to see it all go flinging back to his brother! His useless waste of a brother!

What could Frederico do? Hobble off to battle?

No! He could not protect them! He did not have one straight bone in his body and was therefore completely useless for anything.

Could he withstand the rigorous demands of a king? The long hours, the deep contemplation, the ordering people about and making all run smoothly? No! He was incapable.

He was ugly as well! Snarling ugly! A brute! There were few people in the world who did not shriek in terror the second they met him. How did he believe he would inspire the people? He was nothing to look at. A simpleton. A crippled, wasted use of a person. No villager would wish for such a king.

No one would fight for him or go to battle for him. They would certainly not pay their taxes or anything else they were expected to do—as was the royal family's right to make them do. This whole kingdom would go to complete ruin within a fortnight.

Urgh! Marcus stepped forward and slammed his fist into the highboy dresser in front of him. The pain was dull compared to the loathing swimming within him. His brother—his worthless, grotesque brother deserved to die.

Ha! He glanced toward the ceiling. The irony was that they had been celebrating his death all these years—truly it was remarkable. Especially when the festering pig was living here, gorging himself off their wares, pilfering what he could—stealing from his own family. All the while they turned a blind eye—allowing him to live—and pretended he was dead. The traitor.

It was time—more than time—to rectify this situation.

He picked up the small statue of his father—the one Mother had insisted he keep in the king's chambers—and, weighing it in his hands, he allowed it to bounce up and down a few beats before he hurled it through the window closest to him. The glass shattered—its glittering fragments no match for the heavy weight of the old king's replica. With satisfaction, Marcus watched the thing flip and fall several feet before slipping out of view.

There. There, now *that* was a better place for his father's likeness. He had never enjoyed looking at it.

The sharp breeze of the morning swept into the room and Marcus glared at the broken window. "Thomas!" he shouted. "Thomas!"

A short, pudgy man ran into the room. "Yes, Your Majesty?" He bowed low.

"My window is broken. See that it is fixed immediately. I do not appreciate the chill wind that has been streaming through it."

Thomas's mouth gaped open as he beheld the shattered pane.

"What are you staring at? Fetch someone to fix it this instant. Do not stand about gawking like a child. I want warmth back in my rooms again."

"Yes, Your Majesty." Thomas bowed once more and scurried out.

Slamming the door shut, Marcus spun on his heel and began pacing the floor again. His mind traveled back to all that gold they had collected this morning. He smirked. There was so much they could do with it—ah, perhaps it was not a bad thing his brother was alive a bit longer. Perhaps not a bad thing at all.

His eyes gleamed. More. He needed more and *then* he would kill him!

He stopped and put his hands on his hips. If there was some way he could weasel the girl and his brother into coming up to the tower again, he could get his gold and then have them both hung for treason.

He rubbed his mouth a moment, pondering the proper way to go about doing such a thing. If he took the girl, Frederico would most likely do something rash. They needed to believe he was not on to their plan. He needed them to trust him—meanwhile, while they were creating the gold, he would be preparing the henchmen for their hangings at dawn.

This time, he would not give her warning. This time he would enter and seize them both.

He just needed something to nudge them both to do all he asked of them. What leverage did he have? What would bring her to him—bring them both out of hiding? He paced a few moments more before he halted and whirled toward the door.

"THOMAS!" He shouted so loud the chandeliers rattled. "THOMAS!"

The man hurried into the room, panting and stuttering. "Yes—yes, Your Majesty! I am here." He bowed low.

"Bring me that fool, Mr. Sloat! It is time he pays for his lies."

CHAPTER NINETEEN

RUMPLE CAME INTO THE room, his arms heavy laden with oodles of food.

"My goodness!" Aubrynn exclaimed as she rushed forward to help him. "How in the world will we ever eat half so much? Let this be a remembrance for later—you like to eat!" She was so busy helping him unload the mass that she did not see the stress upon his features straight away. "Indeed, I fear you have brought enough to feed a small army." Chuckling, she followed him to the crate with the silver tray upon it and helped set down the bread and cheese bundles she had taken from his arms. "So, what did you bring for us?"

Rumple set the rest of his load on the ground near the crate, his heart hammering as his mind raced. How would he tell her? She needed to know. "I bring bad news, actually."

Aubrynn's hands stilled in the midst of opening a bundle. "The king?" she asked.

He cleared his throat and then turned to face her. "Yes."

"What has he done?"

"It is your father. The king has removed him from the holding cell and chained him up in the dungeon."

Aubrynn dropped the cloth, her hand flying to her mouth. "What do we do?"

"The king has sent word, through the servants, that he wishes to speak to us both in his throne room immediately or your father will die."

No. She shook her head. "We cannot go there! It is most likely a trap."

Rumple shrugged. "Do we have a choice?" He walked a couple of paces away and looked around the room. "It was obvious, as well, that he knew we were here, since the message was addressed to 'that filth living beneath my kitchens.'"

"He is such a charming man."

He headed toward the makeshift dresser. "Gather the food you would like now and eat as much as possible. It may be your last meal for a while." He rummaged around until he pulled something out of a small, chiseled box. "We will each take two stones with us in case we need to use them to flee. Tuck one in your petticoat, or somewhere the king will not think to look, and keep the other close by." Stepping forward, he handed her the two stones. "Have you found something to eat?"

"I really do not believe I could eat much right now."

He looked at her worried features, his hand going up to brush her cheek. "Aubrynn, all will be well, I promise you."

She nodded and closed her eyes briefly, resting her cheek in his palm for a few seconds, before stating, "Let us hurry. I cannot have my father's death hanging over me."

"He will not die."

"No. He will not."

By the time Rumple led her to the king's throne room, Aubrynn was a complete jumble of anxiety. She placed her trembling hands behind her back and clutched the small pebble as tightly as possible. They paused outside the door as the servant went in the room and announced their attendance to the king. Aubrynn could not even glance at Rumple, she was so terrified of what might happen once they were inside. Her heart beat a wild tattoo at the thought of losing either of the men she cared for most. Though, what the king may do to the renegade Rumplestiltskin she could not possibly fathom—her thoughts were anything but positive.

"You may come in. The king will see you now." The servant held one hand out.

As Rumple and Aubrynn walked into the spacious, marble-floored room, the king sat up a bit taller in his ornate gold-and-red-velvet throne. Two guards stood at attention in their full court uniforms on either side of him. "My, my, my. Look who has decided to grace me with their presence."

Aubrynn curtsied deeply, her dress splaying out around her. With her head lowered, she did not see that Rumple refused to bow. "Your Majesty," she whispered as she stood back up, her gaze taking in the splendid columns around the king's raised platform. So this was where their tax money was going—to richly decorate such rooms. Her eyes wandered to the multifaceted chandeliers and tapestries, to the immense, glorious paintings and the gold-and-mahogany filigreed ceiling. The whole room gleamed in hues of reds and golds. It was splendid, but much too extravagant for such a small kingdom.

"Come here, maiden," the king commanded. "Come all the way up to me."

Rumple began to walk with her, but the king pointed at him. "Filth! You will stay away from me! You will not bring your curse any closer to this throne."

"As you wish." He smiled, glad to know his brother was afraid of him.

With great trepidation, Aubrynn bravely took the last of the steps up to the king. She went to curtsy again, but he held a hand out. "No, do not. Come here, my dear. I want to see you."

She took another step forward as his hand came to rest upon her shoulder. His throne sat a foot or so higher, and so she had to look up to meet his gaze. After a few moments of silence, she finally asked, "Yes, Your Majesty?" She was not sure if she should remain quiet longer, but she was not willing to stand there and look the fool.

His hand snaked up and caught a lock of her long hair. Tugging, he pulled her a bit closer until the toes of her slippers were flush against the marble step where his throne rested. "I forget how beautiful you truly are until I see you again."

She flushed and looked away.

"Aubrynn Sloat, I have warned you before, when your king demands your attention you give it to him—fully."

Her eyes met his cool stare. "Yes, Your Majesty."

"I was not going to speak of such things, but I have changed my mind. I know your game, maiden."

When she did not respond, he continued, "I know you are secretly after my throne."

She balked and shook her head.

"Do not pretend with me! I know you wish to rule with that wasted rubbish over there! You think you can overturn me. You think you can upset all I have done and take over! I think *not*!"

"No! Your Majesty, I promise you. I want nothing of what you speak of—

nothing! How would such a thing even be possible? Why would you imagine this of me?"

"Aubrynn, shut your mouth!" He tugged her hair, pulling her face next to his.

She winced but remained silent.

"Leave her alone!" shouted Rumple.

"Honestly?" King Marcus smirked as he watched his lame brother hobble up to them. "Do you truly want to do this?" He snapped his fingers. Both guards pulled their swords out at once. They stood by the king, awaiting his next orders.

Rumple paused, his hand tightening around the stone. "Let her go. She has no idea who I am. None. She is not the threat you believe her to be. It is me you wish to see gone from this room, not her."

"No, Rumple!"

"Silence!" the king hissed in her face, spittle splattering all over her cheeks and forehead as his hand tightened its grip upon her hair. Anger laced through every word as he continued, "You call this wastrel Rumple? You have a pet name for such a twisted pile of refuse?"

When Aubrynn did not answer, the king pulled her hair, shaking her head. "Answer me! Why? Why do you call him Rumple?"

"I—I—it is because—" Not sure what to make of the king and his volatile ways, she was at a loss as to what to say. What was he really asking of her?

"Because?" He yanked her hair, and Aubrynn could not hold back her cry of pain.

"I warned you!" shouted Rumple. "Unhand her now!"

The king snapped his fingers and the guards lunged forward.

In the blink of an eye, the stone in Rumple's fist shimmered blue before the guards' swords flung across the room to his waiting hands. Shocked, the guards stumbled back as Rumple cautiously moved forward. He was crouched slightly, the swords pointing menacingly at the men. One was pure steel and the other glowed blue from the stone in his hand.

"I said to unhand her," he hissed, his eyes never leaving his brother's face.

Slowly, one by one, the king's fingers unwrapped themselves from Aubrynn's hair until she was free. He pushed her toward Rumple. "I want nothing to do with you and your witchcraft! Stand back!" he shouted.

"Oh, dear, King Marcus," Rumple said slowly as he walked closer. "I think you do want my witchcraft." He grinned. "In fact, I think that is what you want more than anything else in this world."

Aubrynn's heart raced as she scrambled to get behind one of the pillars and away from the men.

The king gulped and then tilted his head in acknowledgment. "You clearly have the upper hand for now. What do you want from me?"

Rumple never let his eyes leave his brother's, though he knew exactly where Aubrynn was. He could feel her—his heart taking in every frantic breath of hers. He had to do this—he had to save her. "You will release her father with a public apology, and then . . ."

"And then?" asked the king.

Rumplestiltskin took a deep, silent breath and said, "And then you will marry her, or I will slay *you*."

CHAPTER TWENTY

"NO!" AUBRYNN'S SHOUT ECHOED around the room. "No, Rumple. No! You cannot make me marry him. What are you saying? You know I love you." She rushed up and tugged on his arm.

If she was not careful, she would ruin everything. Rumple ignored her and glared right at the king. "So, will you do as I say—release her father and marry the girl?"

The king looked incredulously at her. "Do you really love him?" he asked, not quite certain he was hearing correctly.

She lifted her chin and said, "Of course I do. He is more man than you could ever wish to become."

"Careful, my dear," Rumple said quietly, his eyes never leaving his brother. "You do not want to upset your king."

Looking from one to the other and seeing the emotions flit across her face, Marcus was astounded he was witness to such an inconceivable conversation. "Do you really prefer *him* to me?" he asked her.

"Yes!"

He blinked at her fervent looks. "Why? He is so—"

"Do not dare call him ugly! He is not ugly! He is beautiful. He is ten times more beautiful than you will ever be."

"Aubrynn, enough," Rumple commanded.

"And you honestly do not know who he is?" the king asked.

She stepped closer. "No. Who is he? If you know, will you tell me? He refuses to say."

Marcus flicked his gaze toward Frederico, his eyes narrowing. "You really do love her, do you not? You have truly found someone to love the hideousness that you are and so you love her. So much so, you would do anything to protect her. Even hide your true name from her and give up her hand in marriage—to me."

Rumple flinched.

The king laughed. "Oh-ho! Is this not one of the most bitter schemes you have ever heard of? A cursed, crippled fool falls in love, but gives her to the wicked king so that she may live."

"Enough!" shouted Rumple. "Do we have a deal? Or do I end you this instant?" He lunged forward, bringing one sword up to Marcus's throat.

The king grinned. "I would be more than happy to wed the woman I had intended on marrying anyway. We shall do so tomorrow."

"No!" Aubrynn cried and flung herself across Rumple's arms.

He almost lost one of the swords in the process. It scraped across the king's neck and hit his royal velvet robes. This would not do. "Guards!" Rumple called. "Take this maiden to the chamber King Marcus has prepared for her, so that she may calm down and begin preparations for tomorrow."

The guards stepped forward and glanced at the king for his approval. When he nodded, the men strode toward Aubrynn. She stepped back and turned to run, but it was too late. They were excessively quick and caught her.

"Release me! I will not marry him! Release me!" she cried. "Why are you doing this, Rumple?"

The men dragged her out of the room. When the door shut, Rumple stepped away from his brother a bit and Marcus asked, "What will you do now?"

"Nothing. Stay here. Make sure you protect her and treat her well—act as her guard."

"You truthfully plan to attend the wedding? You are eager to watch her wed another?"

"I cannot give her what you can. I cannot even give her a proper home. But you will—and you will treat her kindly as well. I will see to that."

"Aww, the poor little prince who is dead—what would it be like had you been on this throne now? Hmm? You could have wed her, could you not?"

Rumple raised an eyebrow. "Are you really dimwitted enough to goad me into killing you?"

"Ha!" Marcus flicked his wrist. "You honestly believe you have it in you to rule this kingdom all crippled like that?

Besides, if you were truly going to slay me, you would have done so already."

"If you harm her, I will kill you. Mark my words."

Marcus sneered and then shook his head. "It is disgusting, you know?"

"What?"

"I am the king! I am the one with all the looks, I rule the land and own a remarkable castle—and yet you are the one who falls in love first."

Rumple grinned. "It was destined to be, little brother."

"It is mind boggling is what it is."

"Perhaps." He shrugged. "I am sure she will forgive me in time. Soon, she will barely remember me—as you all prefer as well."

Marcus shifted on the throne. "We are only having this little chat because you hold the rapiers. Do not think you can act this way forever. You will not rule over us. You will not demand things and declare this or that. You will not think yourself better than us. You are nothing! Nothing!"

The sword in Rumple's right hand glowed even brighter blue than before, and Marcus felt himself being lifted off his seat.

"What is this? What trickery are you playing at? Put me down at once!"

"Do not forget who has the witchcraft in their possession, and be grateful I am as forgiving as I am."

The king crashed down onto his throne. "Fine! I will do whatever you wish. I will keep her happy and coddled. Brute! You can even have our first child, if you are so inclined. Anything! Just stop doing that hovering nonsense."

Rumple tilted his head, his eyes concentrating on a spot beyond the king's chair. "I would love to have the child. I would love it more than anything. To raise a piece of her—and to truly have such happiness around me." He shook his head. "But, no. I would not do that to her. She will need him much more than I."

The king lunged for the blue sword while his brother was distracted. Whipping it out of his hands, he crowed, "Ah-ha! I have captured the magic!"

Rumple's fist turned blue and the sword immediately found its place back within his hand. "You were saying?"

"Go, now! Be gone with you!" said the king. "I have things to do to prepare for the wedding tomorrow."

"Will you really be there tomorrow, or will you turn craven at the last possible second and flee?"

"What?" he smirked. "To wed the only woman you have ever loved? I would not miss this for all the kingdom."

"Good. See that you are there."

***

RUMPLE WALKED INTO HIS room and threw the swords on the floor at the foot of his bed. He collapsed, sitting on it, his hands immediately going to his face.

What had he done?

What had he done?

His shoulders shook for several minutes as he wept.

He loved her more than he had ever loved anyone—and now he was giving her up to the most selfish of men. But what else could he have done? The second he left her side, the king would have killed her. Marcus would have. He still was not wholly convinced she did not know who he was, and he would not take the risk that she would one day try to become queen. Putting her on the throne, making her *his* queen, was the only way to truly save her life, to guarantee that his brother would not poison her or something worse.

How he hated himself. How she must hate him!

He lay down on the bed, staring up at the stark ceiling. His life would forever be like this now—dark, cold, barren. He closed his eyes.

How he loved her! How he wished in a million ways that things could be different, but he simply could not see a way out of it. He could not.

He would show his face tomorrow. He would wear his finest clothing and stand back with the servants and watch the beautiful girl walk down the aisle and pledge herself to his brother.

And then his world would truly end.

But she would live—and to have her live was worth it all.

Was it not?

CHAPTER TWENTY-ONE

AUBRYNN PACED WITHIN HER chamber. The finely decorated room with its purple silks and cream-colored linen did nothing to satisfy her broken and most distraught heart. How dare Rumplestiltskin do this to her. How dare he react this way and tell her—nay, force her—to marry the king. King Marcus deserved to be fed to the crocodiles of the wildest of kingdoms. That man was a complete, useless muddle. What woman in her right mind would even look twice at such revulsion? He was hideous! Monstrous! Evil!

Urgh!

She spun on her heel and grabbed the first of the many lavish pillows she could find. Holding it to her mouth, she shouted and screamed great frustrations into it for several minutes. Eventually, her shouts turned into sobs as she fell onto her rear end near the bed—the pillow still hiding her face.

Why? Why would he do this to her?

Did he not love her?

Did he not care for her at all?

Was this a polite way of detaching himself from an overly excited girl?

She was so mortified. So very tormented. So torn and lost and scared.

She was more scared now than when she felt she or her father would die that first night. Now she knew she would live—and forever be miserable.

Oh, how she hated Rumple at this moment! How she despised him for being so, so, so—Urgh!

In a swirl of skirts and anger, Aubrynn stood and began pacing again. She needed to see him. She needed to speak to him and make him see reason. Or know for herself that, indeed, he did not love her.

She could not—she would not marry such a man as King Marcus. She would not.

Folding her arms, she looked blindly about the room. It was, most likely, one of the most beautiful rooms she had ever seen, but she did not care.

Inhaling sharply, she turned her head and stared at the tall, intricately carved dresser, then closed her eyes. *Be calm. Think.* There had to be something she could do—but what?

Her eyes fluttered open, her mind anywhere than on the small blue stone she was looking right at, but not seeing. In fact, it was quite a few moments before she recognized and noticed the rock at all.

When she did, she gasped and quickly walked over and picked it up. Clutching her fist tightly around the stone, she began to think of Rumple.

"Take me to his room, please. I must speak with him."

Her hand began to glow that same eerie blue and then—flash—she was gone.

Whizzing through the intense tunnel of light, she arrived inside the room within seconds.

It was dark, so it took some time to catch her bearings. She could hear him muttering something, but she was not listening to what he was saying. Her hand reached out and touched the stone wall—she must be near the door, and he must be lying upon his bed. Just as she was about to announce her presence, she heard—

"But I had to! I had to tell him to marry her, or Marcus would have killed her. I know he would have. And then what would I have done without her?" No matter how many times Rumple repeated the same words over and over again, they did not make any of this easier—nor was his heart any better than before. It hurt. Everything hurt!

He looked up at the ceiling. "Why did I have to be born into this family? This horrid, awful family! Why must my brother rule so cruelly and be such an evil, wicked man?"

He yanked his hands through his hair, causing it to go every which way. "I am glad they do not see me anymore. I am glad I do not have that name! I would never want to be associated with such people ever again. If I were still whole and Frederico, not thought to be dead, then perhaps now, after I have learned this horrible lesson, perhaps now I would be a good king and bring this kingdom the peace it deserves. But now—now it is all ruined. The only hope they will ever have is the goodness of Aubrynn's heart. She—she will give them something. She will help them. At least I could see to that. At least I could guarantee that my brother did not restrict her there—but, oh, what torture to witness her wed to him. What awful twist of fate is this? What—?"

Aubrynn did not need to hear more. Her hands shook as the stone began to glow brightly within them. With as much speed as possible she willed herself out of his room and back to hers. Once there, she walked over to the nearest armchair and collapsed upon it—her legs too shaky to support her another moment.

Rumplestiltskin was the dead prince!

No wonder he would never tell her his name.

Frederico, the poor boy!

She gasped. It was the royal family who cast him aside and announced to the kingdom he was dead. *My word!* Every year since, all the kingdom had come up here and pretended to care for the dead, selfish boy and his ruthless family.

She rested her elbow upon the arm of the chair and held her mouth with her hand. The bright purple and cream and gold colors upon the carpet at her feet swam before her as tears filled her eyes. Their muted shapes dipped and swirled to create a dull gray as she imagined the terror he must have faced at going from a bright, pampered prince—the heir, no less!—to being treated as garbage, filth, and waste just because he was crippled. It was not fair.

How did he manage? How did the small boy cope?

Wiping at her tears, she sat there for some time going over each and every moment she had spent with him these last few days. Her heart soared at the goodness and love she recognized in him. She would have never known he was from the same family had she not overheard him—but he was.

She sat up. He was not just from this family. Frederico was the true king.

Blinking for several moments, she allowed that fact to sink in.

It explained so very much. Why Rumple feared for her death—knowing his proper name meant she would become an easy target. The king would have to kill her to keep his secret.

The animal.

The cruelty.

She shook her head and stood up from the chair. For the first time, she was eager to face them both tomorrow. A servant had said the king had a gown made for her, and it was hanging in her closet now. Slowly, Aubrynn walked toward the closet. Opening the door, she smiled.

Her hand touched the delicate fabric of the gown. It was remarkably exquisite. With a small sigh, she pulled it out. She would wed a king tomorrow—gladly wed him! But it would not be the one they were expecting.

CHAPTER TWENTY-TWO

THE NEXT MORNING BROUGHT a bustle of maids and servants lighting her fire, carrying in breakfast, adorning her hair, helping her dress, and causing all sorts of fluttering within Aubrynn's chest. Everyone said the whole kingdom was abuzz with the news that she would be marrying their king. They were all thrilled he chose her and had been waiting in anticipation for the announcement of their wedding.

The ceremony would be at noon. It was nine and already her father had come, dressed to the hilt, to slap her on the back and announce how immensely pleased he was.

"My heavens! I knew you had it in ya to turn that straw into gold—I just knew it. And I knew ya would find a way to truly capture that king's heart as well. Well done!" He chuckled, quite pleased with himself. "Though, I did not think there for a bit ya had succeeded. Yeesh! Gave me quite a fright to be hauled about into the dungeons like that! It hurt." He grunted and then smiled again, nodding his head and saying, "Yes. My daughter will be queen! Brilliant! Just brilliant!"

"Thank you." Even she did not have it in her to correct or scold her father. He was alive. He may not be any smarter than he was before, but he was certainly still here—and that was a blessing indeed.

By the time he had finished with his boasting and going on about the greatness of their family and left, it was nearly eleven. Aubrynn took a deep breath and ran her hands over the striking gown. She stood in front of the looking glass and grinned back at the woman before her. The cream color brought out her complexion and her hair shimmered in the daylight. She felt very pretty.

A maid came into the room and curtsied. "Milady." She pulled out a single white rose in full bloom with a matching ribbon and a note fastened to it. "I was asked to give this to you."

"Why, thank you." Aubrynn took the rose and asked, "Do you know who sent it?"

"No, milady."

After the girl left, Aubrynn unraveled the ribbon and pulled off the note. Her heart warmed as she read the words:

Aubrynn,
I hope you can forgive me. I will love you forever, but I know this is for the best.
I give you both my felicitations.
Love,
Rumple

She held the note close to her chest and smelled the flower. Oh, how wonderful a change a day made. She simply could not wait to get married now!

***

RUMPLE HELD HIS BREATH as Aubrynn came into the throne room and began to walk down the walkway toward his brother. How glorious she looked! How perfectly wonderful. He had never seen her appear so fine before—she simply glowed. He attempted to stand a bit taller to catch her eye, but she did not glance his way.

She must be so very upset with him.

But she did not seem upset—in fact, she was clearly smiling.

The room hushed as she neared. Every one of the villagers was excited and eager for this happy moment.

By the time she made it up to Marcus, even he was joyful. He must have loved the way she looked in all her finery. The minister began the service with a prayer, as was custom. Marcus and Aubrynn bowed their heads, and Rumple had to strain to hear all that was being said.

Once the minister had begun the king's part of the service, Rumple almost fled. No longer could he watch on impassively—no longer could he brave standing there. And then they began Aubrynn's part. He froze, watching her serene countenance as she stared at Marcus. How he wished it were him she was staring at.

His stomach dropped and his heart stopped beating altogether when the minister turned to Aubrynn for confirmation. No!—he wanted to shout—Say NO! But he did not. Instead he watched in horror as her mouth opened and she began to speak—

Aubrynn took a deep, cleansing breath, and while staring directly at the king, she spoke loudly and clearly for the whole room to hear, "I will marry the king—the true king is the man I love, and it is he I pledge myself to at this time. It is he who is to be my husband. Not this man."

"No!" Rumple rushed forward, the audience turning in shock, some shrieking in fright at the sight of his ugly, bent form hastily staggering up the aisle.

Aubrynn pointed right at him. "That is the man I love!"

He kept hobbling toward her. He must stop her now.

The whole room erupted in a noisy roar, and yet, Aubrynn remained louder still—

"He is the true king! He is Frederico Baldrich Layton!"

Rumple paused and crumbled to his knees about ten feet from her. *She knows! She knows my name!*

Gasping as one, the congregation grew silent.

"This man," Aubrynn continued, now pointing to Marcus. "This man is an imposter. All these years he has been lying to you. He knew his brother was still alive, and yet he played you all for fools while his brother, Frederico, has been goodness divine—he has been kind, generous, and caring. He is the direct opposite of the man who rules you now. Frederico is the true king in heart. And though his body is not perfect, in my eyes, he is. I love him."

In that instant, the whole room began to radiate bright blue. It was so bright, many had to shield their eyes and hide their faces.

The witch from all those years ago appeared before the assembly. Her twisted and haggard old body slowly began to transform, and within moments, a stunning young woman with long, raven-black hair and green velvet gown stood before them. She announced clearly, in a voice like smooth honey, "Now that this royal family has learned their lesson and the real king has found his true love because of his generous and kind heart, I shall remove the curse. Their love has been declared publically by this young woman—therefore, he shall no longer be enchanted." She pointed one elegant finger at Rumple. "May I suggest, Frederico, that you guarantee your wicked brother be kept busy the remainder of his days?"

When Rumple nodded, she grinned. "Good. Enjoy, my boy. Know that all is as it should be now. You are truly deserving of all you have. You have most definitely proven yourself worthy of such a fate. Farewell." She turned toward the crowd, her arm extended. "I present to you, your true king!"

Before anyone could react, she waved her hands and mumbled incoherently. The room instantly turned a flash of brilliant blue once again.

When it was over, the witch was gone and Frederico stood before them in perfect health.

He was tall. He was handsome. He was free.

Aubrynn's jaw dropped. She could not react. She could not think. She was numb.

The old queen, Rumple's mother, was the very first person to speak. "Frederico, is it you?" she asked from the front of the room. "Have you truly come back to us?" She hurried forward, but Rumple did not see her. He strode strongly and purposefully up to Aubrynn—the woman he owed his whole life to.

She stepped back, her eyes taking in his healthy, much larger form. When he stopped right in front of her, she had to look up nearly eight inches just to meet his gaze. "Rumple?" she asked. She had always believed him to be handsome—but now, now it was almost too painful to comprehend. He was stunning—nearly too handsome. It did not seem right to have him so.

He knelt down upon one knee in front of her, his fingers clasping hers, and looking up, he said simply, "I will always be your Rumplestiltskin, if you will have me?" He then brought her hand to his mouth and kissed it.

Those lips, those soft beautiful lips upon her skin. Her arm instantly exploded with the sensation of a thousand kisses racing up to her shoulder and down her spine. It was most definitely her Rumple. When his gray-blue eyes sparkled up at her, she could not help it. "Yes!" she cried. "Yes. It was you I pledged myself to in this wedding anyhow."

The minister pushed a frozen Marcus aside and asked Frederico, "Do you promise yourself to her?"

"Of course I do."

"Then I seal upon you the covenant of husband and wife. You may kiss your queen."

The room roared to life.

Aubrynn moved up a step to stand by the throne and tugged him to stand below her. Their eyes were almost even again. Almost. He was still a bit taller, the menace. Wrapping her arms around his flawlessly strong and straight neck, she brought her forehead to his and grinned. "You may be way too attractive for your own good, but you better still kiss the same, or I may have that witch transform you back."

Without wasting a breath, Frederico swept her up in his arms and proved he could kiss every bit as wonderfully as Rumple did.

When he began to remember the audience all around them, he pulled back a bit, their arms still around each other. Shaking his head slightly, he just stared at her.

"What?" she asked. "What has put such a look upon your face?"

"You."

"Me?"

"Thank you for seeing me. Thank you for marrying me. And thank you for risking your life to do so."

She grinned. "I love you. You risked your existence for mine. 'Tis only fair to do the same, my dear."

"Tilly was correct." He chuckled in disbelief. "She always said those stones would change my life. She was not jesting—they did. They brought me to you."

"And a good thing they did, too! What would I do without you?"

He raised an eyebrow. "So, previously, were you saying you were attracted to me? The new me—Frederico?"

"I am saying that just because you are pretty does not mean you get to treat me any differently than my perfect Rumplestiltskin did."

"And by not treating differently—you mean not kissing differently, correct?"

"Obviously, my dear."

"Good."

And with that, he swept her up in his arms again and kissed her quite thoroughly for all the kingdom to see how a true king behaves with his queen. For no king and queen truly in love will ever halt at just one heart-stopping kiss.

***

HIS ROYAL MAJESTY, KING Frederico Baldrich Layton, and his beautiful bride, Her Royal Majesty, Queen Aubrynn, and their four children ruled together for many years in extreme peace and happiness. They were forever abundant and generous with their gifts and saw to it that all the villagers in their kingdom were handsomely blessed as well. Each family received a new and spaciously built home, with their own attached relieving room.

After the wedding, Frederico made sure his brother, Marcus, went directly to work within the castle walls. There was only one punishment he knew that would torment his brother most. And so, Frederico had him oversee the melting of the gold and creating the coins to be distributed among the people. What sweet irony to have to watch all those glistening coins going forth out of the castle and into the hands of those most deserving of it all.

To be safe, Rumple—for his dear queen still insisted upon calling him that—guaranteed there were at least two guards stationed around Marcus at all times. Not protecting him, of course, but protecting the people's gold from *him*.

When he was not sulking, or not sweating and miserable within the dreaded heat of the castle furnace while creating the coins, Marcus could be found curled up upon a straw bed in a cellar under the kitchen, surrounded by his old wooden toys and landscape windows.

The queen died shortly after the wedding, and no one remembered to mourn for her. Though to be fair, Aubrynn did have Frederico's old headstone done over and the queen's name carved onto it, and allowed her to be buried in the exact same spot of ground where she had told the world her son was.

Aubrynn's own father had to sober up, for there was a declaration sent throughout the land that the king's gold could not be spent on ale or other strong drink. That must come from their pockets alone. And since Aubrynn's father had not a job of his own and a farm to run without a daughter to do so for him, he found himself having to buckle down and work the land again—thus tilling and creating the necessary means to contribute to society once more. Since his daughter was the queen, he was expected to be the greatest example in the community. He eventually became a prosperous landowner and had several of the younger lads working for him, and finally retired as a satisfied old grandpa, bouncing young princes and princesses upon his knee and telling those children the great tale of when his daughter, their mother, proved to the kingdom she could turn straw into gold.

The End

Also in the Jenni James Faerie Tale
Collection:

Cinderella

CHAPTER ONE

ELLA PICKED UP THE last basket
of clothing, her arms strained from
attempting to carry the heavy, wet mass
the twelve or so feet to the drying line.
Thankfully, her stepmother had the
gardener place the line closer to the house
and in its shade, due to the sun fading her
clothes, or Ella would have had to walk
even farther from the washing room.
Most fine houses used the drying lines
inside, but Lady Dashlund preferred to
have hers outside on warm days, so
making the work twice as hard for Ella.

As Ella shook out the last of the
petticoats, she overheard her stepsister
Jillian shriek.

Oh, dear. She probably saw a mouse.

Ella sighed and quickly snapped the lacy fabric onto the line. Tossing in the remaining pins, she picked up the basket and ran toward the large manor home. No doubt they would all be in an uproar and upset if they could not find her.

Another shriek rang out, loud and shrill, as Ella slipped off her outer shoes in the entrance near the servants' quarters and hung the wet apron to dry on one of the wooden pegs mounted upon the stone wall. She could clearly hear her stepmother shouting by the time she managed to wrap another clean apron around her waist and head up the servants' stairs.

Brushing and smoothing her dress with her hands as she went, Ella tried to remain calm. That summer, it had been especially difficult to keep the mice population down. The whole kingdom suffered from the vermin, and her stepmother and stepsisters seemed to take the sight of them the hardest. Ella was the only one of the four brave enough to try to catch them, and she had better do so quickly before her stepmother's temper got the best of her family. That was all she needed—Lady Dashlund in a foul mood. Then the whole house would pay for several days.

As she rounded the corner into the large, immaculate corridor, her feet tread upon the fine, lush carpet her father had chosen. The sumptuous rugs from the Orient lavishly displayed throughout the rooms were one of the final improvements he had made to the house before he passed on a few years back. Her heart lurched. Oh, how she missed that man. How there were days when she truly needed him near her.

Ella approached the drawing room and attempted one last time to make herself presentable before she entered. She was rather surprised to hear joyous sounds coming from within. Taking a step into the room, she beheld Jillian and Lacey laughing quite loudly and dancing about together like small girls.

Finding her stepmother across the way near the rose-colored settee, she walked up and curtsied. "Is there anything I can do for you? I heard the shouting and came as quickly as possible."

Lady Dashlund shooed her with a wispy white handkerchief, a rather large smile upon her face. "No, no. We are not in need of anything. We are all quite elated. You are welcome to continue with your chores—we will call you when we need you."

It was then that Ella noticed the small missive in her stepmother's hand. They must have had some good news. Curious, but not willing to risk Lady Dashlund's wrath, she simply said, "Yes, milady." Ella nodded, dipped into a short curtsy, and turned to go.

"No." Miss Lacey Dashlund halted in mid-twirl and put her foot down to catch her balance. "Ella cannot go just yet. We *do* need her, Mother. *Think*—the duke is coming here in only a few minutes. We need everything to look splendid! He is coming! He is coming! And this time—this time I shall finally secure him." Lacey squealed and shrieked loudly, and then picked up her sister's arm and began dancing about again.

"Girls, enough," scolded Lady Dashlund, though she was smiling. "It is time you freshen up and stop gallivanting around or you will be quite flushed when he comes."

Miss Dashlund twirled Jillian out in a final spin and then giggled with her as they stopped their play. "Oh, is it not the most glorious day?" She smiled and waltzed her way to the settee, clasping her mother's hands within her own.

"Yes. It is." Lady Dashlund grinned at her daughter before turning toward Ella. "Will you please let Cook know to send up tea as soon as the duke arrives, and make sure she adds a little something special—something to make him stay this time."

"Yes."

"Oh, and when you are through, please sweep off the front step. We do not want him walking up to the house when it looks such a sight."

"Yes, milady." Ella curtsied again and rushed from the room. She would have to be quick to clean off the whole of the front steps before the duke arrived. Lord Gavenston rarely came late. In fact, more often than not, he was early.

She hoped for his sake and Lacey's that her stepsister would not blunder this meeting like she had previously. Ella winced. Lacey was always incredibly graceful—unless His Grace was around. And then, quite simply, she became a bumbling buffoon and would somehow or another cause great catastrophes.

Hopefully, this time all would be well. Ella crossed her fingers for luck just in case. After all, the sooner Miss Dashlund was gone from the house, the fewer chores Ella would have to do for her silly stepsister.

***

"OH, NO! YOU ARE not getting me to step foot into that house." His Royal Highness Prince Anthony chuckled as he drew in the reins on his beautiful horse, causing him to stop in his tracks about a half mile down the road that would eventually lead them to Lady Dashlund's rather exquisite manor. The manor, he could tolerate. It was the family that made him shudder.

"But you promised," Lord Gavenston replied, drawing in his rather fine black as well.

Anthony shook his head. "No, I did not. I promised to accompany you on some errands, Cousin. I did not promise to waltz myself into *that* home and be prodded and fawned over like some ninny. Why, those girls could cool the east, lowering the temperature a whole two degrees with their eyelash fluttering alone." The prince ridiculously fluttered his own lashes. They were on the most glorious of roadways, with fine green hills and rows of delicious apple and sturdy oak trees, some of the greatest lanes in all the kingdom, and here he was—looking the fool instead of enjoying the marvelous countryside.

Zedekiah laughed. "You are quite awful, you know."

"I kno-ow!" he replied in a singsong voice, the type reserved for pantomimes.

"And you look like a nincompoop." Zedekiah clicked his tongue and tapped his mount to press onward. "I, for one, would not wish to be seen with you if you are to act this way."

"I cannot. I simply cannot do it," Anthony replied as he tapped his horse as well. "My mother would have my head if she knew I had even spoken to them, let alone stepped in their house—and you know it!"

"This is why I had to sneak you away, so you would accompany me." Zedekiah looked over as Anthony came up. "The queen forces me to run these errands because she and Lady Dashlund were schoolgirls together. She does it to pay particular courtesy to her longtime friend. But she would rather be dead than seen conversing with the woman, which is why I, as the duke, must be her go-between. And honestly, I wish anything—anything—other than this task."

"I pity you, but I cannot risk it. They would devour me in a heartbeat."

"Come! You have not been here for ages—a good five years at least. They may have grown since then."

The prince crowed. "Yes, and this is why you need me to hold your hand. Because they are such proper ladies and behave so well! No, my mother has told me anecdotes about what the family has done to the royal castle alone. I have sheets and sheets written to me of nonsense this Miss Dashlund has done—do you have any idea how much it cost my mother to host them the last time they came? The number of shrubs she had to replace because of that girl's foolishness?"

"Which is why I need someone with me now. I would rather come out of there in one piece!" Zedekiah begged. "Please?"

Anthony stared at him as their horses rounded the corner of the lane. The great house was about forty feet in front of them. He looked up and then reached over, his hand waving his cousin to a halt. "Who is that on the steps?" he asked quietly as both horses stopped.

"I do not know." Zedekiah peered at the girl Anthony indicated. "She looks like a maid of some sort. Why?"

"Because I could swear it is Ella."

ABOUT JENNI

Jenni James is the busy mom of eleven children (seven hers, three her hubby's, and one theirs). She's also the mom of fifty book babies and sixteen screenplays too. When she isn't dreaming of creating new stories, she's chasing her kids around the house. She lives in a cottage nestled in the tops of the Utah mountains with peacocks, chickens, ducks, geese, turkeys and her beautiful keeshond named Holly.

Jenni loves to hear from her readers. You can email her at thejennijames@gmail.com
Or snail mail at:
Jenni James
PO Box 449
Fountain Green, UT 84632

Lightning Source UK Ltd.
Milton Keynes UK
UKHW011020080320
359965UK00001B/1